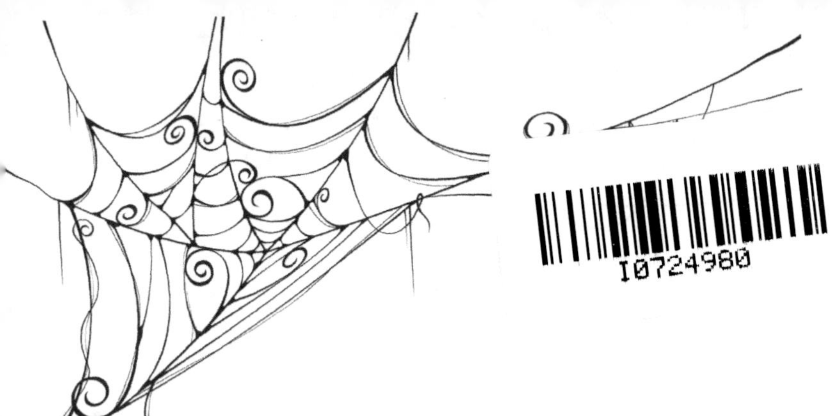

THE SOUL WHO (ALMOST) GOT AWAY

A Grim Reaper Mystery Comedy Adventure

Riya Aarini

1

I dropped off another soul on the other side. It'd been a chatty boat ride, the bubbly soul and I gossiping about the latest fashion trends and wishing 80s retro was back in style. It was rather comforting to know someone else also longed for the return of tie-dye windbreaker jackets. I could've used one on the blustery days, rowing across this frigid river.

On my silent, lonesome return trip, my thoughts wandered as aimlessly as my boat. I had a job many would die for. I met each and every soul who'd ever graced the earth, whether for a few brief minutes, ten colorful decades, or somewhere in between. Admittedly, some were more tolerable than others—I'd rowed my fair share of whiners, grumps, and scoundrels across to the banks of eternity. In general, though, meeting the entire human clan was a unique professional privilege.

I loved my job and performed it with precision. Due to my prompt arrival, no soul had ever lingered uncomfortably in limbo. I maintained my centuries-old boat, sealing cracks and ensuring it never sank with an unwitting soul in tow. My cloak grew increasingly tattered, but who had the time to sew patches with a nonstop schedule like mine? Considering all my stellar achievements, I hoped to win the upcoming Employee of the Year award—it'd be a feather in my hood.

Before I knew it, I reached the edge of the cosmos that led to the Afterlife Headquarters. Taking double steps at a time, I made my way up the stairs and into the two-story whitewashed building.

"How you existin', Pippin?" I said, strolling in.

Pippin was the print room guy. He worked in the basement, engulfed by reams of paper stacked three feet high, eight massive printers, four copiers, and surrounded by numerous scanners. Despite the stuffiness in the air, he dutifully printed up colorful brochures advertising the glories of the afterlife—the spirit guides would hand these to newcomers who stepped onto the banks of eternity for the first time. He also printed coupons with referral codes—refer one soul to the afterlife and receive an extra hour-long dip in eternity's healing springs—with no expiration date. Who could resist a deal like that? The afterlife was big business, and we needed all the help we could get to incentivize souls to come and enjoy their stay.

"Just fine, Reaper," said Pippin. "Finishing up printing this first-time customer coupon. It's meant for souls who've never been to eternity before." He held up a glossy sheet of paper printed with two rectangular vouchers, each of which said, *Good for One.*

"Doesn't that make every soul?" I asked, eyeing the sophisticated print with gold-tone borders and fancy red calligraphy lettering. Afterlife promotions exuded class.

He twisted his lips. "Um, not quite. We've had souls arrive, go back, and then return years later."

"Oh, right. I've rowed a few souls from those near-death-experience fiascos." I pointed to the ceiling with my finger bone. "Someone up there needs to pay more attention."

"Anyway, what can I do fer ya?" Pippen asked, stacking the vouchers neatly in a corner on the large, center white table littered with a mess of staplers, toner cartridges, and glass jars holding scissors. Each table had its own recycling bin—HQ prioritized environmental sustainability too.

"I just stopped by to see if my *Vote for Reaper* stickers are ready. The nominations for the Employee of the Year award are in progress, and I aim to win by a landslide." I made a clicking sound with my jawbone and gave him the finger-bone gun gesture.

Pippin scanned the print room and lumbered toward a shelf with multiple narrow shelving units. He peered into each of them, then pulled out a stack of prints from the third shelf.

"Here ya go. Just printed," he said, handing them to me with his horseshoe-mustached smile.

Bouncing on my toe bones, my response was immediate. "Yep, still hot!" I juggled the papers in my hand bones to avoid feeling the heat.

A few seconds passed before the sticker sheets cooled down enough to handle comfortably. "Amazing job, Pippin." I offered an affirming nod. "Glossy and eye-catching."

"Thanks, Reaper. And good luck on the award." He turned back to printing a series of mystery coupons. Newly arrived souls simply scratched off the silver foil to view their prize, whether it was a sightseeing tour of the afterlife, tickets to the eternal angel choir—made popular by Frank Sinatra's and Bing Crosby's souls being exclusive members—or a cooking class.

I bid him sayonara, and headed back up the stairs.

The office was busy as usual with spirit guides bustling to and fro and Life and Death supervising the whole afterlife affair from their architecturally stunning management offices.

I passed by Cassandra's dull, gray cubicle. Being one of the cheeriest spirit guides, she stood out as a beacon of joy and gave me her customary warm smile. Her cheekbones stayed permanently raised from smiling so much. As her eyes lit up, I stopped to say hello.

"Nominations are being accepted for the Employee of the Year award." I smoothed down my cloak, if only to release some of my pent-up energy. "I made you a little gift so you won't forget to vote."

"Oh? What's that, Reaper?"

Biting down my grin, I handed her a freshly printed black-and-white *Vote for Reaper* sticker, bordered with five gleaming gold stars. A star performer deserved star treatment.

"Vote for Reaper. Making the afterlife better," she said, reading the sticker out loud in her soft-as-a-cloud voice. "Hmm."

"Well?" I asked, my insides vibrating. "Do I have your support?"

"Of course you do," she said. Her sunny, contagious smile made me grin ear bone to ear bone.

I kicked my heels in the air, let out a whoop, and moved on to entice the support of my other colleagues.

"Moe, my man!" I said to the grumpy, old spirit guide who could've used a few pointers in customer service.

"What now, Reaper?" he answered gruffly, gray whiskers flapping with his sharp breaths. He narrowed his gray eyes as he looked me up and down.

Unshaken, I proceeded to satisfy his inquiry. I rested an elbow bone on the edge of his cubicle countertop as he stood next to it. "We've worked together for centuries, from across the river to the banks of eternity, but always toward the same objective: to give souls the best afterworld experiences possible. As I'm sure you know, I aim to be recognized as a leader in my field."

"And?"

He didn't seem phased at all by my ambitious proposal.

"So, your undying support means the afterworld to me." I brought out the sheet of glistening circular stickers, peeled one off it, and stuck it to the breast pocket of Moe's translucent ashen robe.

He looked down at it, feeling the smooth surface with his thick, wrinkled fingers. "What's this?"

"It's a reminder to vote for me for the Employee of the Year award." I flashed him a thousand-watt grin.

Shrugging half-heartedly, Moe grunted and moseyed on.

Gotta love Moe. After watching him scuffling at the ground, I turned my attention to the nearby break room, lured by the sputtering sounds of coffee.

Larry, another spirit guide, poured himself a cup of cappuccino from the espresso machine.

"Pal, friend, comrade," I greeted him with open arms. "Dearest colleague!"

"You obviously want something, Reaper," the spirit guide said, bringing the steaming foam cup to his lips.

"Okay, you got me. I do." Standing as tall as my nine-foot frame would let me, I handed him a *Vote for Reaper* sticker. "Wear this."

His bushy brown eyebrows leaped off his forehead. "I had Pippin print me a bunch of these too. Except, my stickers say *Vote for Larry*." He reached across the break room counter and picked up a sheet of yellow-orange, cheery-as-a-canary stickers.

My jawbone dropped open. "You did?"

"Yeah, I guess we're in for some friendly competition." He handed me a sticker. "I'd never won before, so I thought I'd give it a shot this year."

Seeing it, my shoulder bones drooped. I didn't need stiff competition. Larry was beloved by all, from Life and Death themselves—my esteemed higher-ups—to the countless souls he'd thoughtfully helped navigate through the complexities of eternity. Even I had a soft spot for this modest spirit guide who never made ripples.

His sticker curled in my tightening grip. The sound of the crumpling plastic backing broke the awkward silence.

All I wanted to do was win, and earn the validation I needed to prove to everyone and myself that the reaper was a valued worker, a stellar employee who performed his duties with utmost precision, a phantasmagorical entity still important to the afterlife enterprise.

An award like this contributed to my self-worth, confirming that my work and the way I performed it were valid. It was important that others acknowledged and supported me professionally.

In fact, my identity revolved around each soul pickup and drop off. With little free time to pursue leisure activities, work was all I had. I needed this award like Irish coffee needed cream.

Looking past Larry, I clenched my teeth.

Whatever it took, winning the Employee of the Year award was my top priority.

2

Death ushered the afterlife team into the conference room. Cassandra, Moe, Larry, the other spirit guides, a few cherubs, and I stood around perplexed. He didn't call us together unless he had some pivotal news that impacted everyone in the office. What bomb was the boss about to drop?

I chatted with my colleagues, trying to calm my nerves, though I stumbled over most of my words.

After several minutes of anticipation, Death strode in: a towering machine built of ripped muscle, wearing black slacks and a fitted black polo shirt that accentuated his masculine physique. Everyone stopped talking and turned their attention toward him.

Following the boss came a diminutive, four-foot fellow, bald as a potato and stumpy as a dachshund's legs. He shuffled to the head of the conference room, his round face pale and unexpressive.

Cassandra and I glanced at each other incredulously. Who was this guy?

"Respected entities, valued employees, your attention is warranted," Death commandeered in his sonorous voice, silencing the team. With his dark, penetrating gaze, made darker by his thick, unkept brows, he scanned the room.

The spirit guides, Life, and I arched our necks like swans to look up front.

"The afterlife team is very busy, and has been for billions of years. The death toll never stops. It's solely our duty to guide souls pleasantly and amicably to the next world without a hitch. I am proud to say all of you accomplish the afterlife's mission. But I decided we could use a bit of help to reduce our heavy, nonstop workloads."

Everyone in the conference room turned to each other with wide eyes and *ooh'd* and *aah'd*.

"This is the reason I've hired a new spirit guide." Death glanced over and down at the stumpy guy.

A new spirit guide? I clenched my jawbone. After working with my trusted colleagues for seven centuries, I wasn't too sure how I felt about a newcomer. What was this guy's work style, and would it be compatible with mine? Insecurity grew from the pit of my abdominal cavity.

"Team, I'd like you to meet Stew, the newest spirit guide to help out at the office."

The boss motioned for Stew to approach. Once he did, Death placed his massive arm around the spirit guide's petite shoulders. In fact, Death had to hunch down quite a bit to perform this welcoming gesture.

Stew smiled a little. It was barely noticeable.

"Say a few words, Stew," Death commanded, and stood back with his massive arms folded across his gargantuan chest. He gave the little guy the limelight.

"Ahem…I am deeply honored to join the afterlife crew," Stew started. "There's been much commendation spoken about how efficiently the enterprise runs. As a spirit guide dedicated to upholding the afterlife mission, I pledge to make work easier for all of you fine entities. I am your humble servant." He closed his almond-like eyes and took a bow—a rather odd gesture.

Death grinned from ear to ear, his pearly whites sparkling against his dusky skin. He gave Life a wink. With her pink bubble-gum lips, she smiled back.

The rest of us clapped, welcoming Stew to the team.

"Oh, and I've got a surprise to share with my new, esteemed team members," Stew said.

"What's that?" Death asked.

Stew ran out of the conference room and returned seconds later, carrying a rectangular glass pan topped with swirly, white cloud-like formations that were somewhat burnt at the tips. I arched my neck bones to see exactly what surprise was in store.

"Southern banana pudding with meringue," Stew announced. "Help yourselves. I baked it myself." He stood next to his creation and puffed out his chest.

Well, if the new spirit guide offered us a creamy dessert on his first day, he just might be sweet to work with. I exhaled. As I was about to help myself to the banana pudding, Moe and Larry jumped out of their seats and hurried to the front, beating me to it. They sliced themselves generous pieces and noshed.

"Mm. Out of this world, Stew," Larry said through a messy mouthful.

"Yeah, good eats." Moe stuffed his face, leaving bits of meringue hanging off his gray whiskers.

Life looked at Death, arched her finely trimmed brows, and smiled, as if to say, *What a find!*

The next morning, Stew brought in a batch of soft, freshly baked blueberry muffins with crunchy crumb toppings—the tastiest muffins in the afterworld. My colleagues and I crowded around the break room, taking bites of his amazing breakfast dessert.

"Stew," Cassandra cried out, "you're a heavenly baker."

"Aw, shucks," he replied, as a flush swept across his cheeks. "Wait until tomorrow when I bring lunch."

And the next day, he did bring in lunch: a flavorful, herby taco casserole topped with crushed tortilla chips. It was an instant crowd-pleaser, and brought the whole office together. Stew wasn't only a magnificent baker of sweet treats, he was an exceptional chef of savory dishes.

For dessert, he'd baked classic chocolate chip cookies, a timeless favorite even in the afterlife—that's why they called them *timeless*. Before I could get my hand bones on one tempting cookie, the entire batch was gone, only crumbs left in the handwoven, rattan basket he'd brought them in.

I couldn't help but say to him, "Stew, I don't know your secret, but whatever you put in the food uplifts our spirits—even the crankiest of us, like Moe."

The spirt guide laughed. But I didn't even know it until I glanced down at his face. He was that low-key. He seemed to be approachable, with his flair for cooking and his generous spirit. I could've asked him to vote for me for the upcoming Employee of the Year award. So, I planned to do just that.

I took him aside on a Tuesday afternoon. "Stew, you make a great flan, rich and milky with just the right blend of vanilla and caramel."

"Aw, thanks," he said, shuffling his feet and looking up at me.

"You're a prized member of the team."

"It's an honor, truly." He rubbed the back of his neck.

"You're so valued that even your vote counts," I said.

"Vote? For what?"

"The Employee of the Year award is coming up, and I'd like to ask for your support."

"Certainly, Reaper. I give you my promise." He smiled, almost as proudly as he'd won the award himself.

I shared a happy glance with him.

"But remember awards aren't everything," he said, waving his index finger back and forth. "Too much validation isn't a good thing."

I tilted my skull. How sweet, giving me unwarranted advice. But what did a rookie spirit guide know? I twisted my nasal cavity and made no more of his statement.

"It's just my two cents. I'm sure you'll win. Something just tells me you're a winner."

I dropped my jawbone and pressed my hand bones against my rib cage. Me, a winner? He was too much. Blushing, I laughed and returned to my desk with a light flutter in my abdominal cavity.

With the effortless way this first-rate spirit guide won everyone's admiration, he could've swayed the whole department in my favor. My shoulder bones relaxed.

The award was mine.

Over the next few weeks, not a day went by that Stew didn't bring in a sumptuous treat, a homemade casserole, or a healthy fruit plate splashed with citrus juice.

Cassandra and I stood in the break room, chatting and munching on giant oatmeal raisin cookies.

"He's a real addition to the team," I told her. "Fostering morale and showing everyone he cares." It was true: everyone liked unassuming Stew.

Larry strolled in and grabbed a banana from Stew's fruit basket. "Hey, guys!"

We returned his greeting.

He gobbled up the fruit and tossed the peel, but it missed the trash basket.

Without meaning to, I stepped backward, my heel bone landing on the peel. Before I knew it, I found myself flailing and scrambling to avoid a fall.

It took a minute before I stabilized myself. "Larry!" I screamed. "You trying to make me slip on the banana peel, crack my skull open, and die a second death?"

The spirit guide, with a pained expression, tried to explain. "No, no. Really, I didn't mean to—"

"If I die a second time, that award is all yours." I didn't feel too good about screaming at my colleague, but I erupted spontaneously.

"Sorry, sorry. I—"

In the nick of time, Stew walked in. He took a stance between us, his arms out like a referee but without the whistle. "Gentle entities, you're colleagues, friends. You shouldn't be fighting."

I stopped my tirade and looked into Larry's tearful eyes.

"Ugh. You're right, Stew."

Collecting myself, I outstretched my hand bone, and Larry, though hesitant, shook it.

With interventions like that, Stew instantly became the team's most valued member. Even when he flirted with gorgeous Life, my eternal crush, at the break room table, I didn't feel a tinge of jealousy—that's how great a guy he was.

A few days later, Cassandra and I munched on Stew's melt-in-your-mouth caramel popcorn. He'd made it at home with his very own popcorn maker. He'd even showed us a picture of the glass contraption with the red accoutrements, which looked like it was straight out of a nineteenth-century carnival.

Crunching on the sugar-coated kernels, I remarked to her, "Bringing all these treats and brightening our days... he's like a little fairy godfather."

3

Given how Stew had made the office so inviting, I almost didn't want to leave to do my rounds. But duty forever called.

I opened my phone and checked the list Death had texted me earlier. We'd resorted to texting, as it streamlined the soul collection process compared to the old-fashioned way of me hauling around a burdensomely long sheet of paper listing all the souls for pickup.

"Bolivia," I said, skimming the list. "Nestled in the Andes Mountains." Traveling to the highland country would be like taking a mini-vacation—as was most of my daily work-related travels.

I scanned the notes for the cause death. "Malaria, unsurprising," I scoffed. Malaria was an insidious disease in Bolivia, afflicting a large percentage of the rural population and causing a host of deaths; hence, the need for my services.

Grabbing my scythe, I hurried to my 10:49:36 appointment. My travels took me across the four thousand miles of the Andean peaks, the longest mountain range I'd ever traversed on Earth. I crossed over the picturesque peaks of Chacaltaya, the snowy Chaupi Orco, and the rugged Macizo de Pacuni.

The morning air was crisp and clean at these high altitudes. The wind dispersed any pollutants from the cities, giving me the joy of breathing pure air for the duration of my travels.

A couple of dark, moving specks caught my attention in the snowy range below. A pair of brazen mountain climbers wielded ice axes as they ascended the frosty Andes peaks. Impressed by their navigational skills, I gave them a thumbs-bone up. They responded by frantically tightening their harnesses, probably to make sure I wasn't coming for them.

On the way to the collection spot, the Amazon rainforest sprawled under me like an enormous mossy green shag carpet. Journeying through swaths of lush trees, from eighty-foot walking palms to the ever-so-useful rubber trees, as well as over endless meandering rivers, was a perk of my job. The haunting mists above the tree line lent the whole area a spooky vibe—right up my alley.

I finally reached Rurrenabaque. As soon as I set foot in the breezy port town, a middle-aged man dressed in a blue-and-white plaid shirt, and wearing a chullo made of alpaca over his head, greeted me with a near-toothless smile. In his local indigenous language, he offered me a jungle tour of the Amazon.

"No, sir, I just came from that way," I replied. "I'm here for Mateo Carlos Gutierrez Flores."

He pointed north with a sun-kissed finger. Grateful for the helping hand, off I went.

Mateo's soul hovered over his body lying on a cot inside his thatched-roof house.

"Dang mosquitos," I said, offering him words of empathy as soon as I arrived. Empathy wasn't in the job description, but I aimed to add a little comfort whenever I could. Dying was hard enough, and a bit of compassion during this once-in-a-lifetime event always helped. "Gotta hate those pesky blood-suckers."

"Yes, Reaper. I tried to flick it away, but I was too late." With a frown, he pointed to the tiny bump on his arm where the mosquito had injected that fatal bout of malaria.

"It'll be all better in the next world," I assured him, leaning in. "Like it never happened."

Scooping up his tired soul, I gave him safe passage to the other side.

"Chau," he said, waving back as he walked into the realm of eternal light and love.

"Goodbye to you too!" I yelled. "You'll love it there!"

As I paddled my boat away, my abdominal cavity started to rumble.

"Hmm. Must be hungry." There was only one place that could satisfy my desire for some good eats: the office—specifically, the office break room that Stew stocked with irresistible, homemade goodies.

I made haste to return to headquarters and satisfy my gnawing hunger. It didn't take too long to cross the cosmos and make my way up the flight of stairs to the break room.

"Just what I need." I rubbed my hand bones briskly, eyeing the counter piled with colorful plates of pizza lettuce wraps and hummus-and-veggie sandwiches.

Choices, choices! My abdominal cavity growled louder.

"Uh, I need something meaty." I shunned the healthy stuff and opted for the deep-dish cheeseburger pizza casserole. The hunk of flaky pastry enveloping the juicy, sizzling meat—hidden inside like a treasure in a sand pit—made my empty insides cry out loud for a sizable helping.

Cutting myself a hefty portion, I devoured it like a wolf that hadn't eaten in three days.

The rumbling in my tummy stopped abruptly, and I let out a long sigh. I felt rewarded, having eaten the tastiest combination of pasta, cheese, garlic, onions, and the star component—meat. I basked in the feeling of a job well done. After all, I'd cleaned the plate of every drop of beefy juice.

I left the break room patting my abdominal cavity when I nearly bumped into Stew. He carried a large tray of a dozen black velvet cupcakes topped with white sugared skull and crossbones. Seeing the skulls made me squirm a little.

Nevertheless, I exclaimed, "Ah, dessert!" and reached out to grab one.

Stew knitted his faint brows and slapped my hand bone.

"Ow." I pulled back. It kind of stung.

"*Tsk-tsk*. This is for Death."

"For the boss, eh? Surely, he won't eat all of that."

"Death can handle more sugar than you think." He turned up his pug nose and walked past as I stared in disbelief, scratching my jawbone.

The boss approached from the water cooler down the hall.

"Stew! Nice to see a hard-working spirit guide looking so chipper."

"Oh, sir, you're too kind. But compliments aren't necessary." Beaming, Stew held out his tray of cupcakes. "See, I made these just for you."

"Great! Why don't you leave them in my office? I've got a meeting to run to, and I'll have a bite later."

"Of course, sir." Carrying the too-good-to-be-true cupcakes, Stew disappeared into Death's empty office.

Gawking as the entire scene unfolded, I figured: at least Death would get dessert.

I checked my schedule. Another pickup within the hour, this time in Singapore. Still craving a sugar rush, I hurried to the exotic island country.

Singaporeans rarely died. Its famed track record for producing numerous centenarians made it a country worth envying. Most of the islanders boasted optimum health, making Singapore the only nation on the planet with the most people who lived to be a hundred.

Naturally, it came as a slight surprise to be summoned there to pick up my next client. But Seraph Huang, a proud centenarian, glamorous in her youth, was on my list.

I traveled past the coral reefs on the shores of Singapore. A macaque snagged a crab and began breaking its shell for a tasty seafood bite. I paid no heed—after all, life and death surrounded me in all forms.

Then, as I rushed through the twisted mangrove forests, lazily bowing their branches into the muddy water, a giant python wrapped around my ankle bone, bidding me to pause. It did all it could to squeeze tightly around my skeleton and suffocate me—but it didn't know who it was dealing with.

Since I had no heartbeat, it couldn't sense when I was dead.

The gangly snake continued to wrap itself around my bones, unraveling its coils, then repeating the process—apparently confused. I finally got tired of the snake's shenanigans and started to unwrap its coils as fast as they kept twisting around me.

With an impatient sneer, I bonked it on the head with my scythe blade. It fell into a momentary daze. I happened to have a travel-size bottle of mouthwash on me—the burning kind no one in their right mind dared to use. I plucked it from my cloak pocket and doused its snake-face. Immediately, the python withdrew and slithered away. Even pythons couldn't stand the burning sort of mouthwash. Why did they even sell it? To repel pythons, of course.

After this minor irritation, I entered town, arriving at a pistachio-colored apartment in a two-story frescoed shop-house in Joo Chiat. Corinthian pilaster decorated the building, along with stucco leaves and brightly colored tiles featuring illustrations of pomegranates and flitting hummingbirds.

Seraph Huang lay on her bed, next to the open window with a view of the courtyard. I approached silently. Her legs looked strong, probably from a lifetime of walking everywhere. Next to her bed, on the nightstand, sat a bowl of half-eaten, whole-grain rice. With junk food priced higher here than nutritious foods, it's no wonder she lived to be a hundred.

In a moment of terminal lucidity, she bolted up, hobbled to the bathroom, and popped in her dentures. Seraph returned to bed and died.

I collected her soul. "You look marvelous," I told her.

"It's all in the teeth, dearie," she replied. "I always wear my teeth wherever I go."

We sojourned to the next world, where she never had to worry about hassling with dentures again.

I picked up a snorkeler in Australia's Coral Bay and one very happy Dane in Denmark. As the workday wound down, I checked my list one more time to see if I'd missed any stragglers.

Upon unlocking my phone, a text popped up. It was from Death. Apparently, he'd updated my list. I jerked my skull back slightly, as I didn't expect any new additions. The workday had already been long, and weariness had overcome my bones.

"Hmm. Jimmy Muffet. California. 20:01:36." In other words, about eight o'clock.

I sighed. No biggie. Just one more pickup. As the summer sun descended, I lumbered off to the good old USA to complete my final collection of the day.

I crossed the famous hunk of red metal, known as the Golden Gate Bridge, in San Francisco. Arriving at the West Bluff Picnic Area, I scanned the beach, looking for my last client.

Maybe he's taking a swim. I waited on the sand, digging my toe bones in. It was a soothing, stimulating sensation as the grains massaged my bones. But he didn't show.

Granted, I was a little early, so I decided to hike up to the Golden Gate Bridge. It being a clear evening, Alcatraz came into sight. I'd collected many a soul from the famous former prison, and the feisty ones never came easily.

I turned my skull. The San Francisco skyline looked amazing from this vantage point. In fact, I enjoyed grand views in every direction. What else could a reaper ask for to close a satisfying workday?

My digital watch showed one minute past eight o'clock.

Still no sign of Jimmy's soul.

My breath grew quick and shallow. Unable to stay still, I searched the beach and picnic area, top to bottom, east to west, every inch of sand and grass I could make out in the growing darkness.

But Jimmy Muffet's soul wasn't there.

4

I began hyperventilating. How could a soul go missing? It wasn't feasible in the otherworldly realm. It's not as if souls vanished into thin air, like duct tape on moving day. They were made of eternal celestial matter—and matter of any sort couldn't be destroyed. Perhaps it'd converted to another form: Jimmy's body into a soul. A soul I intended to collect but couldn't due to mysterious circumstances.

Beads of sweat formed on my skull. I brought out my phone to double-check my list. Maybe I'd misread the date or time or location. I was exhausted. Anything was possible.

Nope, one minute past eight o'clock had come and gone and still no sign of Jimmy's soul. I stood in the precise location, West Bluff Picnic Area, where the pickup was scheduled. It wasn't miles of uncombed beaches, but rather a small area I could quickly survey.

Staring at the ground, I scratched my skull. Surely, his soul had to be around here somewhere. Death never flippantly scheduled collections, but rather put immense effort into the details of every passing. Each final exit was carefully planned, from the location to the manner of leaving the earthly sphere. I could trust the boss's meticulous work.

Hmm. Maybe the soul escaped to another dimension. Honestly, how many dimensions were there? I glanced at my finger bones and began to count: the physical plane, the mental plane, the causal plane—

No, no, no. I shook my skull. I was wasting valuable time.

The Golden Gate Bridge had lit up with a series of golden lights, creating a spectacular vision stretching nearly two miles. Against the shadowy backdrop of the starry night sky, the breathtaking structure rivaled the otherworldly light emitted by souls.

Entranced by the stunning sight, I stood as still as an opossum playing dead.

No, I couldn't stay distracted. I had a soul to collect, and he wasn't here. I returned to ruminating on Jimmy's whereabouts.

After being on the job seven hundred years, there was only one place souls go—to my dimension, where I picked them up and transported them to the eternal realm. It's how the afterworld operation always ran. It was a well-functioning system that didn't need a change.

With jerky, clumsy movements, I continued searching the beach for his celestial form, hoping at least to catch his aura. Night had fallen, leaving me investigating Jimmy's whereabouts in pitch darkness. But souls—made of pure energy—stood out against the night sky like an LED light-bulb in a darkened room.

If his soul were in the vicinity, I had my work cut out for me.

Nine o'clock turned into midnight. Jimmy's soul still hadn't come into view.

My gaze darted in every direction. I grew increasingly aware of my environment, and any minor movement that would've indicated a soul was present.

It got me thinking. I paused.

What if Jimmy didn't have a soul? Maybe he was a cold-blooded Russian mafia hitman who'd immigrated to California for better prospects in trading uranium. Or a callous drug kingpin, working the unforgiving streets of San Francisco. My mind began to spin.

I pulled out my list to check the notes section for Jimmy's occupation. He was a washing machine salesman. His last place of employment was Martha's Appliances, which had been in business thirty years. Death kept track of all this vital information, as it helped stir his creative juices when scheduling the manner of passing. I breathed a sigh of relief. A washing machine salesman probably had a soul.

Yet, the absence remained unsolved.

My skeleton shook uncontrollably from skull to toe bones. This was the first time I had failed a pickup. Guilt started weighing on me. I kept tugging at my cloak collar. My hand bones curled inward. Could I no longer perform my job with laser precision? Maybe being on the job for over seven hundred years was taking its toll on me. Should I retire?

If I couldn't perform my job, what good was I to the afterworld? It was only one missing soul today, but what about tomorrow, and the day after? Death wouldn't be happy about confused souls floating around out of place, haunting the world, and causing chaos. The eternal realm had standards to uphold, first-class customer service to deliver, and a reputation for distinction. An ancient Reaper couldn't stand in the way of excellence.

Slumping, I stared down at my empty hand bones. I loved my job. I enjoyed the privilege of global travel opportunities and the chance to chat up new people every day. I woke up motivated, energized to work. My health was still in peak condition, despite me consisting primarily of ashen bones. I had plenty of precious centuries left in me to continue collecting souls.

I pushed up my sleeves. The reaper wasn't about to hang up his cloak.

Then, just as quickly as I'd boosted myself up, an unwanted pessimism overwhelmed me.

Doubts about my professional competency swirled like a dust storm in my mind. An unfamiliar feeling of self-disgust filled my every cavity.

What would Death say? He'd reprimand me, and I'd cower under him like a puppy being scolded for staining the carpet. I clenched my fist bones and looked up into the starry sky.

Why me?

Plus, I had a performance review coming up. Death would certainly point out this glaring blunder and suggest areas of improvement. How more humiliated could an experienced reaper get? He'd use this incident to point out my weaknesses and say I wasn't meeting expectations. My career was at stake!

Rocking myself, I trembled in my bones.

Even worse, the Employee of the Year award nominations were underway. If my colleagues knew about my failed attempt to pick up the soul, it'd reflect poorly on me. They'd chastise me about my lack of afterworld customer service. "Imagine how lost the soul would feel," they'd rebuke. I'd grow red in the face bones being unfairly scrutinized. My approval rating would drop dangerously low. I'd be labeled an under-performing employee. I pressed my hand bones against the sides of my skull. I'd never win the award!

Jimmy Muffet's missing soul was the catalyst for my downfall. This situation was totally out of control. Where could his soul have gone anyway?

No, no, no. I couldn't let my self-doubts consume me. I was the reaper, and I aimed to get back in control. I'd been doing my job successfully for seven hundred years. All these centuries, I never missed a pickup. Never did I leave a soul in limbo. Each and every soul received prompt and courteous service. I even offered extras, like friendly chats during the boat ride, and helped them onto the banks of eternity.

With a sigh, I plonked down on a picnic bench and let my chin bone rest in my hand bone. As the dawn began to stir, I ruminated on my massive failure, along with my long track record of success. I processed, accepted, and analyzed my rollercoaster of emotions.

What I needed was to turn this bitter failure into a learning opportunity. I'd learn from this utter fiasco, foster a reaper resilience, and grow professionally. If, that is, Death allowed me to keep my job.

I'd tell the boss one setback didn't define my entire career. I'd served the afterlife enterprise faithfully. I deserved forgiveness for one error. In fact, my professional qualities surpassed this one miserable failure.

I pressed my jawbone tightly. A fire burned within me. Fueled by this ugly torrent of negative emotions, I grew determined to course correct.

I sat upright and breathed in deeply. The fresh morning air cleared my mind.

As my rib cage expanded, I sought to take the next most logical step: file a missing soul's report.

5

I sped back to headquarters. What was the proper procedure for filing a missing souls' report? It was a duty I'd never done before. I stood in the middle of the lobby running my hand bones over my skull.

I wasn't even sure if the Afterlife HQ had an office where I could file the report. As I glanced around looking for answers, the black rectangular directory near the front door caught my eye socket. I scrambled toward it.

"Marketing Department, first floor," read the letters in bone white. Nope, the afterlife's marketing team focused on acquiring and retaining existing souls, and building afterlife loyalty. It couldn't do its job right in the perplexing event souls went missing. I shrugged.

Next.

My finger bone slid down the directory. "Printing, basement level." No help there for my purposes.

Leaning in, I continued scanning the various Afterlife HQs suite numbers and floor levels. "Board Room, Conference Room B, International Division." Nope, nope, and nope.

Muttering, I verbalized all the pros instead of the cons of my search. The lobby receptionist glanced at me over her chunky, turquoise cat-frame eyeglasses. I lifted my skull, smiled, and waved at her. She resumed her desk work while I resumed my search.

"Administration, second floor." Life's and Death's offices were listed. Sighing, I scanned past them.

I drummed my finger bones on the directory glass. I clenched my teeth, releasing my pent-up energy until my jawbone hurt. Failing in my task, my throat closed. I threw my arms bones into the air, ready to give up.

But persistence was a reaper's trademark. I gave it one last shot.

Focused intensely, I peered up and down and then, at the very bottom of the directory, I noticed another location listed in tiny print—print so small it rivaled the small print at the bottom of legal contracts. In fact, I could've sworn the listing was scribbled in with pencil. I hunched over and scooted closer to read it, my face bones just an inch away from the glass. Aha! It was the Office of Missing Souls, basement.

Yipping and yaying, I threw my fist bone into the air and leapt, completely airborne for five seconds.

My feet bones landed with a thud.

"Are you all right over there?" asked the receptionist, in her nasally voice.

"Couldn't be better," I replied with a grin. "Well, I could a little, but generally I'm great!"

Now, all I had to do was file the report. It'd be following protocol, giving me the chance to save my job and win the Employee of the Year award to boot. I scurried to the top of the spiral stairs, which would take me to the basement level. As I sprinted down the staircase at lightning speed, it occurred to me the office might impose a waiting period before filing. Twisting my nasal cavity, I scoffed at the idea. Jimmy's soul should be reported, even if I wasn't sure if he was missing. Time was of the essence.

I reached the basement level, passed by the print room, and poked my skull inside.

"Hey, Pippen!"

Standing at the giant laser-based copier, emitting the mega level of heat of a controlled nuclear fusion, the print guy turned. "Oh, hello there, Reaper. What brings you down here today?"

"Oh, the business of souls. You win some, you lose some," I said, with a bowed skull. Somewhere along the way I'd definitely lost Jimmy's soul.

"Gotcha," he replied with a wink and a click of his mouth.

I dashed down the dim, dusty hall, checking the various office labels. The Office of Missing Souls didn't appear, even as I neared the end of the hallway.

My gaze turned watery.

But one final door lay ahead. I slowed my pace as my chest cavity heaved. The door stood in the darkest area of the hallway. I wiped away the cobwebs covering the door label. "Office of Missing Souls. Bingo."

I grasped the brass doorknob, my hand bones tingling, and twisted it. The knob turned, albeit with gargantuan effort. The door croaked loudly as it opened. A musty, ancient odor whacked me in the face bones. Clearly, the office hadn't been used in centuries, if ever.

The office appeared dimmer than the dreary hallway outside. Coughing, I waved my hand bones across my face bones to avoid breathing in the thick whirls of dust I'd disturbed upon opening the door.

Behind several teetering stacks of paper on a small desk, an entity came into sight.

Ah, a staff member. I stepped toward the personnel—the only one in the room—while gazing at him.

"Ahem." I stood in front of the tiny desk, my stance wide and my shoulder bones back.

A wee voice, coming from a wee entity wearing black suspenders, round Windsor glasses, and a curled, perfectly sculpted dark mustache, replied. "Can I help you?"

Bouncing from foot bone to foot bone, I exclaimed, "I've been dying to see you!"

Not batting an eye, he didn't seem amused.

"I'm the Grim Reaper, officially known as Reaper. Glad to make your acquaintance. I've never been to the Office of Missing Souls in my entire working career." I glanced around and stroked the head of a crouching brass human figurine. "You should really go for bobbleheads. They'd brighten your day."

He didn't flinch a facial muscle.

I hooted at my own humor, my laughter extending longer than normal. "Right." I wiped the sweat off my forehead bone. "So, I've got a problem."

"Don't we all?"

"He-he. But I've got a special problem. It's unlike any I've encountered before."

"I don't have all eternity," he said dryly.

"I thought you did?" I asked, glancing at my everlasting surroundings.

"Listen, Mr. Grim, or whatever your name is, I've got a job to do, and if you don't hurry up and spill your issue, I'll close the office for the day."

"You actually leave?" I asked, wide-eyed. "The front door seems like it's never been opened!"

He sighed audibly and rested his chin on his hand, glaring like there was no tomorrow.

"Okay, okay." I said with quick breaths, pushing my hand bones in front of my skeleton. "All I want to do is file a missing soul's report."

"You do, eh?"

"Yep, it's what I just said."

"I'll need some information from you." He got up and plucked a sheet of paper from the other side of the desk. He blew on it, scattering at least two inches of dust.

"Fill out this form. I'll need the soul's full name, date of birth, last known location, clothing, and physical descriptors, like tattoos."

"I'm not sure about the last one. Souls generally don't have tattoos. See, they disappear with the body once it passes."

He gave me a glazed look.

"But I'll do my best with the descriptors. I'm sure I can figure it out."

"Also, note whether you believe the soul is a victim of foul play, is senile, or his safety is in jeopardy."

"Jimmy's middle-aged, fortyish, so no senility expected."

The entity roughly pointed to the paper, signaling he didn't care to chitchat.

"He-he. I'll fill this out right away." I grabbed the sheet and took it to the nearby counter and filled out as much information as I could.

Minutes later, I returned the completed paperwork. "You don't suppose a missing soul investigator will be assigned to the case or a cold case advisor to facilitate forensic services, do you?"

"Listen, Mr. Grim. The Office of Missing Souls is on a tight budget. We don't have the funds to keep an investigator or a forensic expert on payroll. Plus, souls typically don't have fingerprints or dental records, neither of which legitimatize enlisting their services. Souls don't go missing every day."

Judging from the suffocating dust and cantankerous nature of this humorless personnel, I didn't think souls ever went missing. But I had a missing soul on my hand bones. And in the rare instance souls truly did go missing, it was a big deal in the afterworld.

By all appearances, this was a mysterious case of a soul who got away.

I returned to my bright and airy office on the second floor with a lightness in my step. After all, I worked in a clean, well-lit environment that encouraged productivity.

"Heya, Reaper," Cassandra said with her usual cheery countenance. "Did you try the fudgy brownies Stew made?"

"Uh, no, I was kinda busy."

"Well, they're in the break room. You should try one. They've got rainbow sprinkles!" she said, pulling her shoulders up to her smiling face. "He's really outdone himself this time."

"Thanks, maybe I will."

"By the way, we didn't get your input."

"Input for what?"

"Didn't you get the text? Larry had sent out a work group chat, asking the team for their suggestions on an idea for possibly improving afterlife protocol. He wanted to run it by the staff to promote the eternal joy of souls in the next world."

"I didn't get the text," I grumbled.

"Oh, you didn't? I thought he included everyone."

My brow bones furrowed. I knew it. Larry was up to no good, excluding me from important discussions to make it look like I wasn't contributing.

I clenched by teeth, feeling a flush grow over my face bones. Larry was intent on sabotaging my chances of winning the Employee of the Year award. It was just like him, an overly ambitious spirit guide, to ruin me.

My nasal cavities flared. I already had a missing soul to contend with, and now I dealt with a spiteful spirit guide out to dash my hopes for winning the prestigious award. I needed that fudgy brownie now.

Breathing fast, I shot up from my chair and stomped like a soldier toward the break room.

On my way, Larry, of all entities, crossed my path. I looked him in the eye—but he didn't acknowledge me, much less glance at me. The spirit guide walked straight past without uttering a word.

A tightness developed around my empty eye sockets. This spirit guide had the audacity to devalue me by not acknowledging my presence! I seethed in my empty insides. This was no narcissistic injury. This was a dire attack on *me*. My defensive armor was full on.

With a loud snort, I trudged into the break room and grabbed the biggest fudgy brownie on the platter.

6

As I chomped on the chewy treat, staring vacantly at the plain break room wall, it occurred to me that Death didn't know about the missing soul. If anyone had to be aware, it was the boss. Souls gave the Afterlife HQ its raison d'etre—without them, there'd be no need for the eternal realm, much less the thriving afterlife enterprise for which Life and Death worked tirelessly. So, protecting the well-being of the dearly departed was of utmost importance. Souls fed the afterlife machine.

Revealing my mistake to the boss would take guts, of which I clearly had none. But I did have skin in the afterlife game—*ahem, not literally.*

Inhaling deeply, I prepared for Death's terrifying roar to blow past my skull, possibly unhinging it from my neck bones. Wiping my jawbone of stray crumbs and ready for my inevitable second death, I mustered myself up from the break room chair. I broke out into a cold sweat as I proceeded on tiptoe-bones to Death's office.

My skeleton shrunk into itself, and I had only rapped on the door.

"Yes?"

I popped in my skull, doing my best to hide behind my hood. "Hey, boss. It's just me. Little ol' me."

"What d'you want, Reaper? You bringing me some all-around cheer, like my new hire?"

"Stew?" I wrinkled my nasal cavity. My expression instantly turned sullen. How could he compare an intimidating, veteran reaper, like me, to a stumpy, rookie spirit guide who baked chocolate chip cookies? "I bring fear, not cheer. Remember?" I smiled to myself, impressed by my spontaneous comeback.

Death grunted and dove his nose into his paperwork.

"Ahem. Boss, I've got a little quandary you may want to know about." I jammed my hand bones into my cloak pockets.

He slowly looked up, his dark, bushy brows narrowing on his chiseled face. His strong, square jawline looked more masculine than ever. A little too manly at my highly vulnerable moment.

"Little quandary?" His strong browbone protruded farther than any entity I'd laid my eye sockets on.

"Oh, yeah, not a big deal to the afterworld at all," I said with a brittle laugh. "Just something went a teensy bit wrong."

Death's dark eyes seemed alit with fire. "What did you do, Reaper?" he thundered. Bits of the textured ceiling crumbled, raining to the carpet.

"Actually, it's what I didn't do. See, um, I lost a soul. I failed to pick him up. That's all. Well, I'll be seeing you." I stepped back, ready to flee, when he growled for me to halt.

"You lost a soul?" His Adam's apple bounced up and down as he questioned me.

"Oh, but it's all well and good. I've filed a missing soul's report with the Office of Missing Souls. I'm sure they'll find him. Quick. Pronto. Nothing to worry about, right?" My mouth went dry.

Death gave me a fiery glare. His lips curled, as if his mouth prepared to hurl curses and criticisms at me.

"Reaper! This is a major dilemma. We can't have missing souls floating around. It's bad for business. How would it reflect on us if Earth were haunted by vagrant souls who should be resting in eternity?"

He rose from his swivel chair, towering over me like an angry giant about to decapitate me, his shadow blocking the daylight streaming in through the window, instantly turning his office into a cold dungeon.

I wrapped my arm bones around my skeleton. My teeth still chattered.

Death pointed with his thick index finger. "You need to find this soul, Reaper. And step on it. Or you'll be hearing about this at your next performance review."

But he wasn't finished. He began launching reprimands at me, left and right, nonstop.

I drew my leg bones together, making myself as small as possible. My skull hung so low I thought it'd drop to my kneecaps. As he berated me, my throat closed up. I couldn't get in a word edgewise to defend myself. Crossing my arm bones over my rib cage was my only possible defensive maneuver.

Still, the color drained from my skull even further than usual. How could he rebuke me so badly for one mistake? I'd been in his service for centuries. Never in that time did I screw up, not once. Couldn't he show the least bit of appreciation?

No, not Death, not now. Here he was, undermining my professional abilities without a filter. My skeleton couldn't crumple into itself any further than it had.

I stood in disbelief. Death had suddenly become the adversary. I couldn't argue with a superior. The boss hadn't even double-checked his schedule for any glaring errors. He automatically assumed I'd messed up, that it was all my fault this soul went missing. I expected more tact from upper management.

I endured the unending onslaught of verbal rebukes. What other choice did I have?

In all fairness, I needed to be treated with respect, not blame and toxicity. A reaper, no matter how grim, never operated well in the harsh environment of criticism.

Death seemed to finish venting, and I relaxed my shoulder bones. But apparently, he only took a break, as he resumed his tirade. Again, I took it all like a banana punching bag in the Muay Thai boxing gym. The boss was the super heavy weight, while I was the scrawny light flyweight.

After I'd been torn up inside, Death finally stopped.

"And make sure you find him!" he bellowed, before shuffling his papers on his desk, seeming as if he didn't know where to look.

"Y-yes, I'll do my best, boss." I walked out, my shoulder bones nearly dragging across the gray pile carpet. I wrestled with the boss's harsh treatment of my innocent mistake, my skeleton shuddering.

I stumbled past several cubicles toward my desk, barely attentive to my surroundings. Things had been going so well until now, and Death was normally a great boss to work for.

An exit plan flashed before my eye sockets: I could escape this whole troublesome ordeal. All I had to do was walk away, forever. But I shook my skull. Quitting wasn't an option. A reaper didn't run at the first sign of discomfort. Where would I find another reaper position? In an alternate universe? I dismissed the pathetic idea. Plus, if I jumped ship, it'd look like I'd accepted blame, when I wasn't so sure anymore.

Slumping into my chair, I grew uneasy about the potential negative outcome about this sordid episode—that one missing soul could cause all future souls to doubt the integrity and efficiency of the entire afterlife establishment.

And all because of me. The spirit guides and cherubs would have their day passing judgment. I'd get zero peer votes for the Employee of the Year award. The paranoia was too much to bear.

I retreated inward to my sanctuary. From that safe space, I analyzed the perplexing situation from every angle.

Never in my seven hundred years on the job had a catastrophic event like this happened. Why now, all of a sudden? A gut feeling told me something was amiss, even if I couldn't pinpoint the reason. I smelled a stinky mackerel.

As I wallowed in my professional woes, Stew strolled past. "Reaper! Have a sweet potato tea cake." He handed me a slice topped with meringue to which I couldn't say no. "It's organic."

"You're too good to be true," I said. "Anyway, thanks, Stew. My insides ache. You know, work-related stress. But your wholesome goody will help."

On my way to my cubicle, I nibbled the cake, letting the orange crumbs fall and leaving a trail.

There was only one way to deal with the gnawing feeling pestering my bones: find out what happened to Jimmy Muffet.

It'd confirm my suspicion that something was fishy. I gobbled up the rest of my tea cake, which left my hand bones gummy as crazy glue.

Grabbing a paper towel on my desk, I wiped my hand bones clean. Death had it in for me. But I was determined to vindicate myself. I didn't know how, but I'd unearth concrete evidence, refute the blame, and clear my name—restoring my rightful reputation. No one messed with the Reaper.

I furrowed my brow bone. I had a bone to pick with this Jimmy guy.

7

Where there's a soul, there's a body.

I swooped down to the beaches of the West Bluff Picnic Area, hoping to spot clues that would solve this unprecedented conundrum. My posture grew stiff with an air of readiness.

The daylight made it easier to see, especially compared to last night's dark shadows. Signs of Jimmy Muffet's soul had to be here. Although, I wasn't sure exactly what evidence souls left behind. It wasn't like they cast off a trail of glowing neon plasma in their wake, allowing me to follow it and nab the soul. I paused, resting my elbow bone on my wrist bone and glancing upward in thought.

Adding a physical substance, like iridescent plasma, to each final exit would definitely move things along, but make the entire passage to the next world messier. Maybe I ought to suggest it to Life, who handled all creation, and Death, who whisked her formations away.

I shook my skull. No, plasma would soil my boat. Besides, I was looking for concrete evidence. A reaper worked with finalities, not uncertainties.

And so, I began scouring the beach. I'd arrived early, before the enthusiastic swarms of beachgoers aiming to catch sight of the sweeping views of the Golden Gate Bridge crowded the beach. On this pleasant morning, with few clouds and bright sunshine, the picnic area would be a major attraction.

I pushed onward in the minimal time frame I had to find traces of Jimmy Muffet's soul. A volleyball net swayed gently back and forth on the lush, green grass. Weathered wooden benches bordered the park. Surprisingly, not one piece of litter flew past.

With a lightness in my stride, this was the most pleasant place to conduct a missing soul search.

Holding my shoulder bones back, I started at the very top of the beach, scavenging the grassy park, picnic areas, and barbecue grills. Who knew, maybe Jimmy's soul hungered for a juicy grilled cheeseburger before heading off to blissful eternity?

I searched and searched as my steps grew heavier and heavier. Nothing but blades of grass met my scrutinizing gaze. My neck bones began to ache from staring down at the ground for over an hour. I paused, rubbed them, and looked up to the blue sky to give my bones a stretch.

I'd combed the picnic area without the least bit of success. The high energy I'd started with lessened to a mere sputter, like a car with no more than an eighth of a tank of gas left and ten miles from a gas station.

But the West Bluff Picnic Area consisted of more than picnic tables and grills. Restless, I maneuvered over to the beach, my heel bones digging deep into the sand with every step. In a few moments, the crowds would arrive, filling the area with bodies I wasn't looking for and leisure activities that would compromise any possible evidence and make finding clues all the harder.

I glanced up at the sky again. Searching for the teensiest clues had drained me. I could barely summon the motivation to continue. What was the point? I'd probably never win the Employee of the Year award, be kicked out of the Afterlife HQ, and hover in the in-between realm, lost forever.

A flat rock appeared. Ah, I'd take a breather and drown in my woes.

As I sat on the rock, sighing over and over like a homeless reaper, I gazed around casually. The Golden Gate Bridge looked so demure in the morning, a stark contrast to its stunning, bold appearance in the sultry night. You'd think they were two different constructions.

At the edge of the beach, the ocean waves rolled in, and the whimsical washes of the dramatic yellow sunrise grew stronger. It was a calming place to end my career. Sighing, I began to accept that a piece of myself was about to be lost.

Out of the blue, something very orange caught my attention.

"Eh? What's that?" I dropped my jawbone. It had escaped my notice. My skeleton perked up, and I followed my urge to head toward it.

Flat on the sand, as if it'd been carefully planted there, laid a pair of bright orange pants.

Hmm. Maybe this belonged to someone who'd taken an early morning swim in the ocean. I glanced around, not seeing anyone kicking or floating in the water. No one was in sight anywhere in the vicinity.

I scratched my cheek bone. Finding a pair of neatly laid pants on the beach was rather odd. I crouched down to take a closer look. It was a pair of men's pants. Grabbing the garment, I examined the label.

It read XL. I sucked in a quick breath. Only a man standing six feet tall, possibly two hundred pounds, wore an extra-large size. The notes in my list described my client's height. My eye sockets bulged.

This might've been a clue!

Where there was one clue, there were sure to be others.

I rolled up the pants and left it on the sand. My senses grew heightened.

Visitors started arriving at the beach, laughing, cajoling, and setting up their food at the picnic areas and grills. I couldn't survey the beach any further. I kicked at the grass.

But I could wade into the water, where no one had yet entered.

Wasting no time, I waded in. The water rose up to my rib cage. I struggled to keep my skull high and dry, when a small fishing boat floated past—with no one on board.

I did a double take.

An abandoned fishing boat? In the Pacific Ocean? And this close to the beach?

Something didn't smell right, and it wasn't the giant kelp surrounding me.

My skeleton froze momentarily, and I began to sink. Gathering my wits, I began dog paddling toward the fishing boat. My first assumptions were right: I didn't see a fisherman or a catch of fish for that matter. The vessel had been completely abandoned, and a fine one it was too.

Perhaps the boat had sprung a small leak, and the fisherman swam back to shore and left his pants on the beach. I slapped my hand bone against my forehead bone. Ugh, a pantless fisherman is unlikely in these parts. But I was in California, so anything strange and avant-garde was possible.

My cloak dripping with heavy ocean water, I hoisted myself onto the boat. A life jacket hung off it. A life jacket with no life boded ominous news.

Scratching my skull and gazing out at the water, I tried making sense of this nonsensical situation. Just then, my eye sockets caught something floating nearby. I pressed my fist bone against my jawbone. I had to act quickly before it disappeared beneath the waves.

I dove into the water, cannonball style, and paddled toward the object.

My breath hitched.

It was a phone. No one these days would go anywhere without this essential device. I stared out blankly.

Someone, somewhere, had gone missing. Could it be my client, Jimmy Muffet?

My bones tingled with unbearable discomfort.

As I treaded the water, phone in hand-bone, another object, humungous, long, and gray as steel, surfaced nearby. It looked like a lean whale that hadn't eaten in a while yet still managed to grow to over four-hundred feet. Covering my brow bone to shield my eye sockets from the sun, which could distort objects at sea, I peered at it. My skull jerked back. This megalith was no whale—but a submarine!

I examined the enormous steel vessel. On its side, it read, JL-3 SLBM. My chin bone trembled. A Chinese submarine. But off the coast of California? I shook my skull. No, I wasn't imagining things. The sub kept surfacing, water falling off its sides like a waterfall, until half of it emerged above the water.

That's when I noticed a striped blue shirt fluttering off its flag pole—above the red flag of China.

This got weirder by the minute.

My curiosity consuming me, I dog paddled like mad toward the submarine and climbed onto the top. Inching my way across the slippery surface, I reached the shirt and sighed.

I attempted to pull it down when a naval officer yelled out, "Hey, what're you doing there?"

Suddenly, I felt rooted to the spot. Shuddering, all that came out was a squeaky, "Who me?"

"Yeah, you," he said gruffly. Clearly, he wasn't the friendly type. He marched toward me, his hunky shoulders bowled over, like he was about to throw my bag of bones overboard.

"I'm just, uh, collecting this fine shirt you have here." I grinned sheepishly. "It really belongs *below* this beautiful Chinese flag."

The officer eyed me.

My breaths burst in and out. But I seized my chance.

"Uh, you didn't happen to pick up a fisherman, or maybe a washing machine salesman, about six feet tall, two hundred pounds, did you?" I asked.

"No." He glared, his thick, black brows so knitted they appeared as a unibrow. I jumped out of my bones.

"Well, I'm sure you don't mind if I take this shirt off your hands, do you?" I began hastily undoing the knots securing it to the flagpole.

As I fidgeted, I had a good look at the shirt label, initialed with the handwritten letters *JM*.

"That property belongs to China, you hear?" the officer growled. "We found it first!"

I didn't need him to tell me twice and let go of the shirt. I'd gathered all the information I needed.

"Well, nice meeting you too. I'll be seeing ya!" I leaped off the submarine, into the water, and paddled as fast as I could back to shore.

Wet and weary, I climbed onto the beach and collapsed. The picnic area had grown crowded.

Picking myself up a few minutes later, I thought to investigate the parking lot to look for signs of an abandoned car, but it had gotten too packed with vehicles to make headway. It didn't matter. I'd grown preoccupied with making sense of the bizarre collection of evidence that had surfaced this morning.

A pair of pants neatly laid out on the beach—and bright orange, as if meant to attract, rather than repel. An abandoned fishing boat with a lifejacket hanging off it. A smartphone in the water, and a blue striped shirt tied to a flagpole on a Chinese submarine.

I deliberately lowered my skull, studying the ground and letting the bizarreness I'd stumbled upon circle in my mind.

Then it hit me. I snapped my finger bones.

All this pointed to a disappearance, a drowning. Perhaps Jimmy had gone for a swim, leaving his pants on the beach, but decided to go fishing and swam to his boat bobbing on the water. Climbing aboard in his swim trunks, he figured a good swimmer like him didn't need a life jacket. He hankered for a tan, so he took off his shirt. Somehow he fell overboard, losing his phone and shirt in the water. The Chinese submarine picked up his shirt as a souvenir but never saw his phone amid the waves.

My theory had gaping holes. I shoved my hand bones into my cloak pockets, rocking on my heel bones.

This case and the peculiar details surrounding it kept me stumped. If Jimmy did drown, there'd be a soul hovering over the Pacific, waiting for my arrival.

But not a soul in sight.

I drew in a breath and held it before exhaling, tapping my foot bones against the ground. I pressed my jawbone together. Someone had to know something, maybe his friends or family.

Springing into action, I left the beach and bounded toward the civic courthouse to look up the public marriage records. After taking a quick ride in a charming vintage streetcar, I stood before the intimidating, four-story whitewashed building. I gulped. Given the years of images of redacted documents to go through, this could take ages.

I ran my search at one of the computers, bracing myself for an all-nighter at the courthouse. But inspecting the long list of public indexes didn't take long before I hit gold. My eye sockets softened.

"Bingo. Anne Muffet, spouse of Jimmy Buffet." Ha, what an accomplishment. Nothing ventured, nothing gained. With a clap of my hand bones, I noted their address and sped off to Jimmy's digs.

It was a quiet San Francisco neighborhood. Grecian laurel trees lined the sidewalks, and luxury cars sat parked on the streets under the clear blue, sunlit skies. I trudged up and over hill after hill, as rows of pastel-colored houses seemed to rise sharply higher than the ones next to them.

Out of breath and clutching my heaving rib cage, I reached a flat neighborhood—where Jimmy's home stood—and sighed in relief.

"Okay, 5323S Grant Avenue," I said, gazing up at the three-story Victorian home with crème-colored lattice-work along the windows and balcony. His house appeared so old that I assumed it had survived the 1906 earthquake. I'd been engulfed with that one, collecting over three thousand souls.

I leaned my weary skeleton against the base of the stairs, not keen on climbing them after traversing the endless rolling hills, defying gravity at every incline, and feeling my bones work doubly hard on the steeper ones.

But I had a job to keep, a professional reputation to uphold, and an Employee of the Year award to win.

Huffing and puffing, I climbed up the series of steps, crossed the porch, and knocked on the front door.

I smoothed out my cloak, drenched in sweat, trying to appear collected. Maybe whoever answered would help make sense of the odd collection of evidence. I crossed my finger bones behind my spine.

A muscular woman, who at first glance probably could've lifted seven hundred pounds like it was a down pillow, came to the door. She didn't flinch at the sight of me. Rather, I gasped and took two steps back on seeing her five-foot-ten frame, her intense demeanor as rough around the edges as that of an Appalachian backwoods-woman.

She narrowed her eyes and looked me up and down.

I froze, despite feeling a crucial need to run. She squint-ed.

"Um, good day, miss," I said, a tremor in my voice. "I'm the Grim Reaper and I'm looking for a soul, not any soul, but the soul of Jimmy Muffet. Might you be his lovely wife?"

"Yeah, I'm Mrs. Muffet," came her reply, abrasive as six-ty-grit sandpaper. "They call me Anne. What d'ya want?"

My skeleton shook uncontrollably. "My client—your Jimmy—is missing."

"He hasn't come home in three days," she uttered with a scowl, flexing her bulging biceps.

As my chin bone quivered, I dared to explain my vis-it. "That's why I'm here: to find his soul. Might I come in and have a word with you, perhaps get a little information about his possible whereabouts?" I came across as a little too politely British than usual—but when situations de-manded it, I delivered.

Anne opened the door wider. "Come on in. Have a seat in the front room."

I sighed and entered.

She pointed to a bright orange couch. What was it with Jimmy and orange? I took a seat in the sunshine streaming through the bay windows, twiddling my thumb bones and bouncing my knee bones.

Anne disappeared for a few minutes before returning with a laptop. "This is Jimmy's laptop. Maybe you'll find something on it. I ain't too savvy with technology." She handed it to me.

"You're in good company. We recently revamped things at the Afterlife HQ, upgrading to the latest technology, after all these centuries of relying on paper. I've just gotten used to my phone." I gave her a meek smile and opened the laptop to see what I could find.

My skeleton perked up. "Hmm. The browser's been cleared." I moved my skull closer to the screen. "It was cleared on the day his soul was scheduled to be collected. I find that odd. Do you find that odd?"

"Oh, yeah, I find that very odd. Jimmy was an odd guy."

"Then he synced it to the cloud." I wrinkled my nasal cavity. "He even took photos of his passport." As I continued to snoop, another piece of suspicious activity appeared. "What's this?"

"What?" She leaned her husky body over my shoulder bones. "What d'ya find?"

"Jimmy transferred a boat load of money into a foreign bank account in Eastern Europe." My eye sockets widened.

"Impressive, considering he worked as a washing machine salesman."

"That sneaky sun of a gun."

I glanced off to a corner of the room to process the unfolding of this peculiar series of events. Judging by the flat tone of her insult, I had to ask, "Anne, were you and Jimmy happily married?"

She threw her head of stringy blond hair back, slapped her thigh, thick as three stacks of French toast, and laughed like a jackal. "Jimmy and me? Ha! We go back two years. We'd been married only that long. He'd found me on an online dating site when I lived in Appalachia. He seemed nice enough, clean-shaven, a full smile, and had a thing for orange. So, I took a bus to California and married him."

"Ah, we all make good decisions."

"I had a fine life before Jimmy came into it. You know, Reaper, I once thru-hiked the Appalachian trail?"

"You? I'd never imagine."

"Yeah, all by myself, in a pair of high-top sneakers, with only cans of sausages, bottled water, a pocket knife, and a plastic shower curtain. I'd spent too many rainy nights under that thing. I'd walked through weeds up to my neck too. Still have a few scars from the scratches." She pulled down her collar and pointed to her neck. "It was a nightmare. I wouldn't do it again, like I wouldn't marry Jimmy again."

I jerked my skull back. Here I was, thinking all along that this manly woman could've picked Jimmy up like a baby and done away with him somehow, but he clearly wasn't the best husband.

"Being married to Jimmy was a gom-mess."

"Oh?" My voice rose in pitch.

Twisting her nose, she said, "He just had this strange fashion sense. It bothered me."

"Aha. That explains the orange pants and the striped blue shirt. I agree, a horrible style choice."

I recoiled, picturing Jimmy in his tacky outfit. Silence filled the room.

"Anne, I've got to confide in you. Based on all the suspicious activity surrounding the time of his disappearance, Jimmy might or might not be dead. If he were dead, I'd have found his soul."

"You reckon he's alive?" She leaned in, her eyes as big as saucers.

"I don't know." I stood up, having obtained enough information from her.

"Well, if you find him," she said, bringing up her shaggy, masculine arm, at the end of which was a clenched fist. "You tell him he's got somethin' comin' when he gets back."

A nervous laugh escaped my jawbone.

9

A passport, foreign bank account, and a cleared brows-er meant one thing: Jimmy didn't want to be found.

I ambled down the steps, my mind whirling with possibilities. If he'd run off to Eastern Europe, what compelled him to, and why there?

Then a gripping question popped into my mind like a fresh corn kernel popping—the answer might send me in a new direction.

From midway down the stairs, I spun around, leaping back up two steps at a time. I knocked on the door again.

Anne opened it right away.

"Listen, Anne, one more question."

"Uh-huh?"

"Did Jimmy have any unusual contacts before he disappeared?"

She glanced at the foyer table, picked up a small paper object, and handed it to me. "He'd been seeing a medium before he went awol."

I took the business card. "Thanks, Anne."

A medium? A medium's specialty was to connect with the dearly departed and serve as a messenger between this world and the next. That's right up my alley. I should have this mystery solved in no time. As I proceeded down the steps, I glanced at the card.

Madame Katerina stood out in bold, maroon English letters in the center of the beige card. But the rest of the information was written in Russian.

"Hmm." I rubbed my chin bone, looking blankly at the gibberish. Then I pulled out my phone and opened the translator app.

By now, I'd traversed a downhill slope in the hilly downtown Bay Area. With brawny construction workers resurfacing the streets and numerous smaller crews repairing the sidewalks, the traffic grew congested. In every direction, cars stalled bumper-to-bumper on the steep roads. Drivers sweating under the California sun lay on their horns, wiping their brows and grimacing.

A bicyclist sped past me, sending the folds of my cloak flying. "Hey! Watch where you're going," I yelled at him. But he was already a quarter-mile ahead.

Colossal red-and-silver buses maneuvered through the dense infrastructure, creating conditions ripe for potential collisions. A bright yellow cable car chugged slowly past. Surprisingly, air remained breathable, despite the rush of vehicles and exhaust. Hundreds of fashionably clothed pedestrians in dark sunglasses, cross-body bags, and large backpacks walked the intersection with me—just a fraction of the half million that walked it every day.

The sheer busyness of the streets delayed my examination of the business card. I fiddled with it in my cloak pocket. It was all I thought about in between dodging traffic.

I kept on my path with a furrowed brow bone, eventually reaching the quiet Golden Gate Park. I sauntered into the Japanese Tea Garden and found myself immersed in the Zen-like environment with minimal distractions. The garden was awash with brilliant green foliage, Japanese maples, reflective ponds, and red pagodas popping up from the tranquil landscape.

At once, I felt present in the moment, embraced and accepted by the stunning natural fauna and trickling water. The Afterlife HQ ought to have one of these on the property. Absorbed in this deeply serene experience, the internal chatter stopped, and I could focus.

Upon reaching an arched drum bridge, I deliberated whether to attempt to climb the famous work of art and still keep my dignity. To my better judgement, I averted it and wound up crossing a steppingstone path. I stopped under a bonsai tree and finally felt at ease to examine the business card. And, so I did.

Since the translator app on my phone was open, I simply scanned the business card. Within seconds, the app produced a translation of the card's contents from Russian into English. Granted, as a worldly traveler whose profession took me to all parts of the globe, I understood every spoken language. It's how I communicated with my diverse stream of clients. Reading a foreign language, however, was a different beast altogether—one I'd had no reason to master.

"Madame Katerina," the app read. My jawbone dropped at the translated text below it: "Medium to the Russian Mafia."

I rubbed my eye sockets to reaffirm what I'd just read. Russian mafia? A heavy feeling grew in the pit of my abdominal cavity. Why would the Russian mafia need their own personal medium? Maybe when the mafia wasn't finished with a goon in this life, they made their threats and followed through *after* life with the help of their medium, Madame Katerina.

A shiver ran down my spine.

What did I get myself into? Self-preservation and the Russian mafia never went well together. Pictures of money laundering in Cyprus and Venezuela, car theft rings in Europe, and gasoline tax evasion flooded my mind. Nausea overcame me, and I had to sit down. But I already was.

Then images of the glitzy, golden Employee of the Year award and Death's angry face flashed before my eye sockets. It'd be a challenge to tackle the Russian mafia, but a reaper wasn't frightened off easily when it came to protecting his career. I'd witnessed many a racketeering over the centuries. What was one more? Inhaling deeply and sitting up with my rib cage out, I pushed onward.

I had to contact Madame Katerina. Since Jimmy had been utilizing her services, she might've had the information I needed to locate his whereabouts.

The app translated her phone number, which I saved to my contacts list.

Without wasting time, I made the call.

The phone rang once before a woman with a husky voice answered. "Privet."

"Hello to you too. My name is, um, Mr. Grim. A good friend of mine referred me to your fine services."

"What friend?" she asked in her thick Russian accent.

"His name is Jimmy." My gaze darted back and forth. "Jimmy Muffet."

"I know man by name of Jimmy. He good client. What you want from him?"

I breathed in relief. "See, he mentioned he'd be traveling to an exotic place, and I lost his phone number. Just like that. Can you believe it, in this day and age?"

"I believe anything." Her voice came out monotone.

"You wouldn't by chance happen to know here he is, would you?" I asked, cocking my skull and raising a brow bone.

Then a pause. An anxious, fear-filled pause. The repercussions of failing plagued my mind. What if she sussed me out and sent the Russian mafia after me? They'd have a ball with my brittle bag of bones. I'd befall a horrible *second* death. I glanced upward to the sky, sweating like a garden hose. Why me?

"I connect you. Just a moment."

Eh? That easily? The tension in my bones disappeared.

I heard a click, then a ringing sound. I waited on the line, barely breathing, as the phone continued ringing with the annoying default ringtone. My hand bones shook holding the phone.

After two minutes of nonstop ringing, another woman picked up. Also in a thick Russian accent, though younger sounding, the woman said, "Plokhoy Bridal Agency, connecting Russia to the world. My name is Duplicity. How can I assist you?"

"Oh, he-he. My hearing must not be right. I misheard you say your name was Duplicity. Only calculating rogues call themselves Duplicity. You mean Felicity, right?"

Without missing a beat, she said firmly, "No, my name is Duplicity of the Plokhoy Bridal Agency. Now, how may I assist?"

"Uh, Duplicity, pardon me." Never in my wildest imagination did I think the medium would transfer me to a bridal agency. The source of mail-order brides? I snapped out of my outlandish theories and thought fast.

"I'm Mr. Grim, a magazine reporter from the USA."

"USA?" Her tone grew upbeat. "Yes, I'm listening."

"We'd love to do a feature on your, uh, bridal agency. Can you tell me a little bit about it?"

"Why should we do feature?" She sounded defensive.

"It'd be great for business. Exposure would drive more men to your agency, leading to massive profits. You know how wealthy American men are."

"Of course, I do. Yes, we proceed with feature." She cleared her throat. "Myself and my brother, Shady, we run agency."

"So, it's a family affair?" I asked.

"Yes, as you say. My brother and I connect beautiful Russian women with men from USA and other wealthy nations. In fact, we had recent client, Jimmy, from America."

My breath hitched.

"Can you tell me more about Jimmy? You know, for the purposes of writing this feature?"

"Yes. Jimmy very generous man, especially with Alena, one of our girls. He send her money, cameras for her to send him photos of herself, and many expensive gifts, like washing machine. Alena ask me why he send washing machine. I tell her it's American thing."

"Very interesting. I'm taking notes."

"He took selfie and send it to Alena. She liked. They exchanged emails for few days. Then he come to Russia to marry her."

I fell back against the bonsai tree. The bark split, producing a crackling sound.

Collecting myself, I asked, "This is all great stuff. I'd love to interview Jimmy for the feature. You wouldn't happen to have his contact info, would you?"

"Yes. I give." She paused for a moment, then read out a ten-digit number, preceded by the number nine.

"Do you think he'd want to return to the States?"

"Jimmy odd man. He like orange too much. But maybe he return. Maybe he like Russia better."

"This has really opened my ocular cavities, Duplicity."

"Excuse me?"

"I mean, it's been eye opening. Thanks for your time."

I ended the call with Jimmy's new Russian phone number in my hand bones.

10

Seconds later, I dialed Jimmy's number. The ringtone went on for several agonizing minutes booming, "Hey? Hey? You still alive?"

I rolled my eye sockets. Ringtones these days. Geez.

Ornamental, multi-colored koi fish swam in the nearby pond, clear as the blue sky reflecting off it. The swift, torpedo-like movements of the yellow ones rippled the water. Whiskered and three feet long, I wondered why anyone would pay up to $20,000 for one of these.

I heard a click. My skeleton bolted upright. He'd picked up.

"Hello?" came a strained, shaky voice.

A flush of adrenaline rushed through my bones. Jimmy was alive!

"Jimmy," I said, my speech rushed. "This is the Grim Reaper."

"The Grim Reaper?" I practically heard his eyes pop, and his mouth fall to the floor. Suddenly, a crash of metal and a high-pitched shriek filled my end of the line. He'd dropped his phone.

My shoulder bones slumped, and my body rested limply against the bonsai tree. I lost him. Figured, I should've come up with a more pleasant introduction. Maybe something like, "Hello, Jimmy, you've just won a travel voucher for an amazing one-way vacation to the United States. How 'bout cashing it in?"

I almost jumped out of my skeleton when he returned, sounding like he was fumbling with his phone. "You comin' for me, man?" he asked, panting and his voice cracking.

I let out a huge breath. "I'm not sure, Jimmy. There must be a mix-up at headquarters, because you sound very much alive."

"Yeah, man, I'm alive as a wood board."

My brow bone arched. A wood board? He wasn't the sharpest tool in the shed.

I grunted silently and returned to my unexpected yet much-anticipated conversation. "Jimmy, you're missed back at home. We'd all like you to return."

"No way, man, I'm lovin' it here. I've got an apartment and one heck of a pretty girl."

"Where exactly is your apartment?" I asked.

"Not sayin', man. But I'm doin' just fine."

Drats. He was tight-lipped about his whereabouts.

A small, Javan mongoose darted past, stopped to look me curiously in the eye sockets, then climbed up my leg bone. I attempted to shoo the inquisitive animal away with my free hand bone. Sneering, I shifted to the side, and the mongoose, no longer vying for my attention, scampered away.

"You know, Jimmy, we all thought you were dead. Headquarters sent me on a wild goose chase, looking for you."

He chuckled. "I did it, man. I staged my own death."

My eye sockets popped. He admitted his grand accomplishment nonchalantly. He might as well have said he'd just learned how to use chopsticks.

He seemed proud of himself, not knowing he had a potential obstruction charge coming his way when he returned to the States. Not to mention, my search efforts nearly diverted me from picking up a few souls. I'd made a mad rush to transport them to the other side in the nick of time. Despite collecting them on schedule, the resulting stress-related aches and pains were no picnic.

Jimmy began spilling the beans, describing every bewildering piece of evidence. "I laid my pants on the beach, threw my phone and shirt into the ocean, and tied a life jacket to my boat."

"A Chinese submarine has your shirt," I interrupted. "You'll never get it back."

"It never looked hot with my orange pants anyway." He continued his riveting account—but never explained his obsession with orange. I shook my head in frustration.

"I got back to shore in an inflatable ride-a-unicorn costume. No one noticed me."

I slapped my hand bone against my forehead bone, producing an audible *thud* that must've been heard all the way to Russia. "Yeah, no one would miss that. How'd you get to Russia undetected?"

"The adventure goes on, man." His voice sounded chipper, as if he'd achieved an impressive feat. To his credit, he did have me and the entire afterlife team baffled for days.

"I rode a rented e-bike I'd stashed in the bushes to a bus depot at the Oregon border."

I shook my skull. That was five hours of exhausting pedaling!

"Man, I was determined. I took a bus to Canada, then a plane to Russia. And here I am."

I sat speechless. He'd just clarified his entire fake death scheme in less than five minutes, while I'd been searching for him for three exhausting days and nights. This mess had to be straightened out fast.

"Jimmy," I said in no uncertain tones. "You've got to return home."

"You kiddin' me, man? Have you seen my wife? She'll clobber me."

"I've met her. She's quite the gal." I almost felt a little sympathy for Jimmy. He had a valid point.

"No, man. I'm livin' the life here in Russia. I've got the girl of my dreams," he said, wistfully.

"You mean, Alena?"

"Yeah, man, the sweetest girl in the world. I wake up at five each morning, zip down to the 24/7 corner flower shop, and buy her flowers. She gives me kisses. We're so happy, we're going to be married."

My skeleton stiffened. "Oh, really?"

"Yeah, man. This morning, I took her to the bridal shop. I spotted a dope orange wedding dress, with a big, puffy skirt and orangey handmade flowers. I asked Alena, 'Will you wear that on our wedding day?' She stared at the dress, wouldn't take her eyes off it. Her bottom lip quivered. Tears streamed down her cheeks. Then she threw her face into her hands and ran out of the store, bawling."

"Unreal," I said, jawbone hanging open.

"Man, at that very instant, I knew she was the right girl for me—the one, my soul mate. She was so moved to tears by that bright orange wedding dress. She loved it as much as I did."

I went completely still. "Uh, Jimmy?"

"Reaper, I'm the luckiest guy alive." He sniffled. "What were you saying?"

My chest cavity dropped to the pit of my empty abdomen. I covered my eye sockets, hating to burst his bubble.

Shaking my skull, I answered with a sigh, "Never mind."

Things seemed to be going well for Jimmy. He was alive as can be, and I had no reason to interfere any further. But he chatted on.

"Alena is a ray of sunshine, my dreamboat of a lifetime. I couldn't ask for a nicer girl."

Then came a pause.

"Only thing is, she asks me to deliver packages of chocolate peanut butter cups all over town. They're all neatly wrapped in white paper and tied with hemp string."

"Is that so?" I leaned forward, paying closer attention.

"Yeah, every single day. It's all I do. From sunup 'til sundown, corner to corner, town to town, all over Russia. I'm a salesman, so I know a thing about traveling. It's no big change for me. But the packages are heavy, like really heavy. I'm a big guy. Still, I'm exhausted when I get back from transporting them."

I scratched my skull.

"But Alena gives me kisses and tells me the chocolate peanut butter cups are for the needy. The treats make their day special. She pinches my cheek and says I'm her angel for delivering them. Man, it feels good to be appreciated. I can't say no. But I gotta tell ya, Reaper, the packages weigh me down."

11

How cute, chocolate peanut butter cups.

I tucked my phone into my cloak pocket. Jimmy seemed like a nice guy, maybe not the brightest crayon in the box, but still. All that mattered was that he was alive and doing well. Turned out, I didn't make a grave blunder after all—I'd just have to let Death know that his star employee still retained his star employee status. Nothing stood in my way of winning that coveted Employee of the Year award. By confirming Jimmy's soul was still very much in his body, I'd untarnished my slightly tarnished reputation. I'd wiped my hand bones clean. Mystery solved.

The sky looked bluer than it had in days. The cries of the California seagulls were music to my ear bones, and I probably wouldn't have minded if the opportunistic birds dive-bombed me for unwittingly wandering into their territory. After a harrowing past three days, I could finally put my feet bones up.

I salivated for an ice-cold beer, straight from the fridge, refreshing to my taste buds. Maybe Stew had whipped up another sumptuous treat. With a chilled beer in hand bone and a tasty snack in the other, there was no better way to unwind. I couldn't wait to tell Death how I'd unraveled this impossible mess.

As I strolled out of the Japanese Tea Garden, a contented smile on my face bones, it hit me like a ton of uranium bricks: chocolate peanut butter cups didn't exist in Russia.

I stopped in my tracks. The country didn't import the candy either, and many of its citizens weren't even familiar with peanut butter, much less liked it. I'd collected countless souls in The Motherland, and never had I come across a stash of chocolate peanut butter cups.

Nearly stumbling over a stone, I flailed my arm bones.

A tightening feeling consumed my rib cage. Something else didn't add up. Chocolate peanut butter cups tiring out a six-foot, two-hundred-pound man?

My mind began to chug like a locomotive. Who did Jimmy know in Russia, besides Alena? I rested my chin bone on my hand bone, steeped in thought. Duplicity and Shady of the Plokhoy Bridal Agency.

I grew restless, unable to stand still. A nagging feeling urged me to check these folks out.

At once, the relaxing images of me holding a beer and kicking back vanished.

I fled the welcoming tranquility of the Japanese Tea Garden and jet set off to headquarters, traversing the endless cosmos, a kaleidoscope of colors unidentifiable to the human eye, nebulas bursting into supernova explosions, and galaxies on course to carefully designed collisions.

I arrived in a jiffy at the two-story office. Racing up the front steps to the building, I pushed through the glass lobby door and sped down the spiral staircase to the file room, next to the print room in the basement. I didn't have the luxury of time to say hello to Pippen. This investigation into Russia's chocolate peanut butter cup fascination had grown urgent.

Life and Death stored all their files here, as they were the only forces who kept detailed records of the living and the dead. Spirit guides acted merely as middlemen to guide souls through the vastness of eternity, and angelic cherubs simply gave hope to life on Earth. Lower-level staff had no business with the contents of the files. But as a reaper with centuries-long tenure, I had access to all afterlife records. It was critical to keep notes on the souls I dutifully collected.

The files had been scanned to digital form ever since headquarters had transitioned to the latest technology. I simply had to run a search through the lengthy database. It'd take minutes rather than years. In the centuries before technology, we were forced to thumb through paper files—a massive pain in the sit bones. I could no longer imagine willfully researching 4.5 billion years of life history recorded on paper. Thank goodness for technology—ubiquitous, even in the afterlife.

Per policy, Life created detailed files on every single life form she produced, from each of the 97,000 species of the tiny, snouted Weevil beetles to the friendly arctic beluga whales and, of course, all varieties of humans, law-abiding and not so much.

She also kept meticulous notes on every influential detail of her creations, such as illnesses and injuries that might've hastened their deaths, as well as joyous occasions, like marriages and promotions that would've extended their lifespans. Who knew married people lived longer than lonesome ones?

She continually updated the files as each life event occurred, making her records current up to the nanosecond. It was a glorious feat, considering Life also simultaneously produced life forms. I could go on admiring her remarkableness, but the enigma of the chocolate peanut butter cups pulled at me.

As soon as I walked in, I was struck by a floral fragrance, like freshly picked peonies. I inhaled the pleasant rosy scents deeply, indulging in its mood-enhancing effects. Life had just been here. Her sweet perfume lingered. Ah, nothing like the sweet scent of your eternal crush to greet you.

I got comfy at the computer, nestling between rows and rows of gray, sliding mobile shelves overflowing with manila files and half-open drawers labeled with yellow sticky notes. There, I began my search.

First, Alena—Jimmy's closest confidant in Russia.

I ought to be able to dig up plenty of dirt on her. I *rat-a-tat-tapped* at the keyboard.

With my hand bones touching my face bones, I gazed at the minimal lines of notes on the screen: Twenty-five years old. Surname: Antonov. Went to high school then started work immediately afterward.

Humph, a clean record. Surprising, considering she sent Jimmy off with the suspect chocolates.

I flinched a little, but moved on.

Next, Duplicity Plokhoy. I smirked just typing in her name. I couldn't get over the irony. Who called themselves Duplicity? It blew my mind. I'd surely expose her misdoings based on her name alone.

Tap-tap-tap.

I leaned back, staring at the screen. All her pertinent information was listed clearly: Duplicity, thirty years old, born in Saint Petersburg as Duplicity Smirnov.

"How about that? She really was named Duplicity!" I chuckled.

I continued perusing the records. Three siblings: Daria, Tatiana, and Lara Smirnov.

Funny, no mention of her brother, Shady. I rubbed my chinbone distractedly. Life took excellent records. There was no chance on Earth she'd miss a major life event like the birth of a sibling or an adoption. I sat with a blank look on my face bones.

I shook myself out of my confusion. Maybe more investigating would clear up matters.

Scanning farther down, a marriage record appeared: Duplicity Smirnov married to Shady Plokhoy.

I fell out of my chair with a crash. Duplicity and Shady? Not brother and sister—but husband and wife?

What in the afterworld was going on? I laid crumpled on the cold tile floor, processing the shock of the unexpected information. Duplicity definitely had something tricky up her sleeve.

With a tingling at the back of my neck bones, I scrambled back into my chair. I dug deeper, this time into Shady Plokhoy—Duplicity's *husband.*

Tap-tap-tap. I tapped the keys on the keyboard, like a freestyle tap dancer in some unchoreographed dance, and pulled up critical data: forty-year-old male, imprisoned for several years, inked heavily to prove it. Born in Moscow. Married to Duplicity Smirnov. Member of crime family.

My skull shot up. The Russian mafia!

Dread filled my empty core. It all came crashing down. Shady wasn't Duplicity's brother, as she'd claimed. Rather, Shady and Duplicity were a husband-and-wife duo, active in the mafia, and operating the Plokhoy Bridal Agency, where Jimmy met Alena, who insisted he transport heavy packages of chocolate peanut butter cups all over Russia.

My jawbone dropped. I didn't believe what I'd just seen. But it was true.

I had to investigate. What exactly were in those packages? Candy? Please. I was as skeptical as someone demanding proof of the afterlife. In fact, I smelled a stinking rat.

I pushed up my cloak sleeves, intending to take a closer look at those "chocolate peanut butter cups."

12

Iplonked down in Red Square, in front of Saint Basil's Cathedral, one of the Seven Wonders of Russia. No concerts, festivals, or exhibitions took place, so the site seemed peaceful. I'd transported the souls of a few holy fools—speaking in ambiguous riddles, dressing in tatters, professing depravity, yet cleverly making a point—from around these parts over the centuries. I never forgot colorful souls.

Moscow seemed like a good place to begin my hunt. Jimmy had stayed mum about his location, so I figured I'd start in the center of Russia and work my way outward. The chocolate peanut butter cups had to be floating around somewhere, especially since he delivered numerous boxes daily.

The cathedral stood as a medley of vibrant colors. Smooth swirls of blue and white, green and yellow, and jagged red and green brought the dizzying domes to life.

Enchanted, I couldn't take my eye sockets off the splendor gushing out from every inch of brilliant architecture.

While soaring over the blue skies of the capital on my way here, I'd been privileged with the amazing aerial view. From the top, the cathedral's eight domes formed a majestic star—unerringly wonderful for a structure built by Ivan the Terrible.

I sat down on the dark cobblestone path, absorbing the magnificence of the cathedral's architecture. Granted, I came here to perform a specific task, but had to cast it aside briefly to observe the stunning beauty of this human-made marvel. If only such wonders were built in the afterlife too.

Since time did not stop for me in the Earthly sphere, I stood up, dusted off my cloak, and scoped out the rest of my opulent surroundings. Gleaming modern city towers vied for dominance on the Moscow skyline, a stark contrast to the old-world charm of the quietly breathtaking cathedral.

It'd take a while to find one of those dubious packages. With chinbone jutted, I stomped onward.

The supertall Eurasia Tower, built of tough steel, seemed like a good place to start. If an international visitor or a local in any one of its offices, apartments, or the hotel had received a package, I'd find it. My hand bones dangling out of my cloak pockets, I snooped around the business district.

At the entrance to Russia's sixth-tallest building, I caught sight of a rectangular package sitting on the front step. It was neatly wrapped, just as Jimmy had said. He must've been here! I bounced from foot bone to foot bone, then abruptly stopped, realizing my awkward jig might cause a scene. Careful to avoid drawing attention, I casually strolled toward the box, whistling a tune yet jittering like a jitterbug inside.

Wrapped in white paper and neatly tied with a string made of hemp, the package sat lonesome under the shade of the expansive, hexagonal metal awning. Must've been to prevent the chocolates from melting. Jimmy had been careful. I smiled to myself. What a guy.

Several passersby strode past, failing to turn their heads toward the solitary package. Leveraging my luck, I mingled among them to get closer.

My hand bones began to sweat. I could barely stop myself from transitioning into a sprint. But a lanky, nine-foot reaper dressed head-to-toe in black had to be wary to avoid unwanted detection.

Just as I thought the package was mine, the front entrance door swung open. A man with a thick mustache, dressed in a fitted dark suit, bent down and picked it up. The glass door banged shut.

I'd missed my chance!

I let out a heavy sigh and shook my skull. What a let-down. I kicked at a stone on the sidewalk. It rolled into a flower bed. That pebble survived erosion. If it could endure hardship, so could I. I pushed on.

There'd be more packages in the vicinity. I stiffened my posture, ready to resume my search and solve this strange puzzle of the weighty chocolate peanut butter cups.

I meandered out of the business district and into a less clustered, folksy area. Corner stores dotted the streets. On entering a souvenir shop, my eye sockets widened. Matryoshka dolls, each wooden figurine decreasing in size, lined the shelves. Exquisite collectible wool shawls in intricate patterns hung on the racks. Lacquer boxes—hand-painted with folk art dating from around the time I started my career—sat like wooden gems waiting to be snatched up and carried home.

Surrounded by a bounty of culture, a lightness filled my bones.

A young man wearing a backpack and sunglasses eyed a birch bark frame in the corner. Under his arm, he carried a package, neatly wrapped in white paper and tied with hemp string.

My skeleton froze. A second chance! With an air of nonchalance, I approached him. I'd simply ask him a few pointed questions, request to see the contents of the package, and he'd agree. I'd solve this unsolvable mystery. Easy as rhubarb pie.

Just as I was within conversational distance, he quickly paid for the picture frame, exited the shop, and disappeared.

My shoulder bones slumped. Drats! Another missed opportunity. My movements briefly slowed.

But I regained focus. I had a goal to achieve, a mystery to solve, a bullseye to target. With neatly wrapped packages all over Moscow, I'd surely get my hand bones on one of them eventually. Undeterred by the two prior flubs, I pressed on with furrowed brow bones.

Rock pigeons waddled on the cobblestone streets, cooing and clapping their wings. A scruffy stray dog bolted past, down a long stairwell toward the subway. I followed, struck by the numerous frescoes and paintings at the station—an underground palace for commuters. The stray sat patiently near the tracks. Three minutes later, a train arrived, and the furry canine hopped on. I got on the metro along with it.

The train conductor announced the next stop over the loudspeaker. The dog sat patiently before the door. The second stop emitted the smells of greasy fast food. The commuter dog lifted its nose, sniffed the salty air, then got off. With nothing to lose, I followed.

Moscow looked different in these quaint parts. Gorgeous fountains spurted streams of water like natural hot spring geysers, yellow blooms lent the lush, green grass cheer, and the clean, paved sidewalks invited me near. I wandered the parks lost, though I couldn't say the same for the savvy metro dog.

Then, out of the corner of my eye socket, a white object appeared on a park bench, wrapped with hemp string and camouflaged by nearby bushes.

I stopped breathing for a second. No one was around. I approached.

Merely steps away, I lunged at the package before anyone stopped me. I wrapped my finger bones around the box, clutching it tightly like it was a long-lost treasure. Ha—the package was finally mine to examine.

As I attempted to lift it, though, the sheer mass weighed heavily in my hand bones. A little too heavy for chocolate peanut butter cups. It took monumental effort to barely lift the several pounds of weight an inch off the park bench. How did such a small, pretty box feel like deadweight?

Out of breath, I hastily untied the hemp string and tore off the white paper.

Inside the steel box sat numerous four-inch, silvery-white metal discs.

My jawbone dropped. "Uranium!"

13

Only one place served as a source of uranium: Russia's nuclear sites.

I sat down on the bench, then stood up again, my thoughts racing.

Opportunistic Russian gangsters had been stealing nuclear materials for decades, motivated to turn a profit by selling them on the black market. To whomever these rogue Russians sold the materials could create improvised nuclear devices.

My gaze darted in all directions, absorbing every blade of grass and manicured hedge in sight. My ear bones picked up the sounds of every quacking duck within range.

Nuclear smuggling was a strict no-no. It could lead to all sorts of potential catastrophes, like instilling fear and insecurity among residents and dangerous radioactive sites. The packages containing genuine nuclear materials were real threats, not some bogus metals that posed little harm.

Mind spinning, I nearly passed out.

Ugh, who else but the Russian mafia was behind this—specifically, Shady and Duplicity Plokhoy. Alena must've been a willing participant in the illegal trade, too, as she ordered Jimmy to deliver the packages without ever opening them. Not the brightest flower in the bulb box, Jimmy complied, huffing and puffing and sweating every day to please his pretty Russian fiancé.

The mafia had Jimmy smuggling packages of uranium stolen from local nuclear sites. Poor guy was being used as a mule. He served as the mafia's courier—without even knowing it!

I grabbed the back of the wooden park bench to stabilize my shaky skeleton. Jimmy was being scammed, sent all over the country transporting stolen uranium. A choking sensation developed in my throat bones. I could barely get enough oxygen into my heaving rib cage.

Maybe a little fresh air would do me good, but I was already amid plenty and didn't feel relief.

My fingerbones like gelatin, I hastily tied up the package and left it on the bench in its original location. A reaper who cared about his professional reputation wasn't about to be seen in possession of illegal goods in a volatile country, where prison cells locked behind three steel doors.

Hurrying to another part of the paved garden path, I paced back and forth, changed direction, then paced again with my skull down and my concerns growing as fast as giant Indonesian bamboo.

I could've just left Russia and wiped my hand bones clean. The oppressive stressors of the past few days would've been lifted. What further business did I have here anyway? Jimmy was alive and kicking with a gal by his side. I choked on a cough.

Jimmy was among the living, and that's all that mattered. His soul remained safe in his body. Death would be delighted to hear it. I'd clear my name of the shenanigans, win the Employee of the Year award, and enjoy continued recognition and respect from my colleagues. Now *that's* the existence.

I let out a deep, gratified sigh.

Jimmy would get married to Alena in a nice Russian wedding. He and his new wife would be crowned and symbolically named king and queen of their own little piece of kingdom in The Motherland. They'd smash crystal glasses—and the more glass shards, the happier they'd be together.

I almost wiped away a joyful tear.

An emcee would run the reception, cracking jokes and hosting games to give the newly married couple's guests endless fun. Jimmy would bask in the enjoyment, the attention, the sheer adoration. At the end of the night, his new wife would sweep the floor, picking up the money their reception guests had thrown to help them start their lovely new lives together.

I glanced up at the cloudless, blue sky. Ah, sweet Jimmy would have the time of his life during his week-long marriage celebrations, at the end of which he'd probably take the biggest bite out of a slice of heavily salted bread—signifying he'd serve as head of household. I didn't need to worry about this nice but dimwitted American who only wanted to feel appreciated.

I felt a tug at my heartstrings, particularly significant since I had no heart.

Sighing, I sat down on an empty bench and dropped my skull into my hand bones. A mix of complex emotions welled up inside me.

I propped my chinbone on my fist bone, like Rodin's famed The Thinker. A long-eared owl hooted, "Who? Who?" torturing my already tortured being. Thrushes sang cheery birdsongs and flitted carefree around my skeleton. The internal conflict besieged me. Jimmy would be happy but naively involved in criminal activities, while I'd return to headquarters and win my award.

What was more important: the euphoric love he'd found with Alena and his welfare or my coveted Employee of the Year award? If Jimmy messed up, just once, I'd definitely be enroute to picking up his soul—and there'd be no mistake this time. The Russian mafia would finish him like day-old bread.

I crossed my leg bones, then uncrossed them several times over the course of twenty minutes. I grappled with my two choices: to involve or not to involve. Each option held potential consequences. My professional responsibility was to act in a way that aligned with my values.

Pressing my jawbone together, I made up my mind.

I yanked out my phone and pressed the ten familiar digits.

"Hello?" came a surprised-sounding male voice.

"Jimmy, it's me again, the Grim Reaper." I sat on the ready, prepared to deliver the news of his life.

"Man, I thought you said you weren't comin' for me!" His voice cracked, increasingly high-pitched.

I lowered my skull. "I'm not, at least not yet, but I've got bad news."

"What could be worse than another call from the Grim Reaper?"

I said not much, and began a lengthy explanation of what was really in those packages. "And it's not chocolate peanut butter cups."

He struggled over his words. "You sure, man?"

"I saw them with my own eye sockets and carried them with my own hand bones."

I calmly explained how the Russian mafia had used him as a mule in the illegal uranium trade. He began to sob uncontrollably. I wished I could've handed him a tissue, or, by the sound of things, a whole box.

"Just when I found the perfect girl!" he cried out, sputtering.

"You better return to the United States," I said.

He argued with me for a half hour in between sobs and snuffles, before finally accepting the truth and agreeing to come back.

"But what about my wife?" he asked, his voice quaking. Clearly, he was more concerned about her than smuggling for the Russian mafia.

"Uh, yeah, well, that's a problem."

I convinced him that he was safer in the States than in his current location. It took more bickering before he finally agreed to leave Alena right away, return to the US, and go into hiding.

Instantly, the accumulating tension lifted from my skeleton. Ending the call, I flopped back against the bench, threw my arm bones out, and exhaled. What a meandering escapade. A moment of euphoric relief overwhelmed me.

After all that, some relaxation would do me good. Maybe a stroll through Moscow's folksy souvenir markets to clear my mind. So, I headed eastward for a few hours of quiet time.

Metal trinkets, handwoven baskets, and solid gray fur caps with ear flaps sat on the outdoor tables or hung on the walls of the makeshift stalls. The markets grew busy as people bustled to and fro. I pulled my black hood over my skull to further conceal myself amid the shoppers.

I wandered into a small corner store selling magazines and snacks. Grabbing a glossy photography magazine, I flipped through the pages, admiring the images of contemporary sculptures and paintings. It was a leisurely way to while away the time.

As it turned out, word traveled lightning fast.

"Did you hear about the Plokhoys?" the burly shopkeeper asked his slender, spectacled customer as he handled the transaction with a brown cigar between his lips.

Amid the musty, barnyard smells in the tiny shop, my ear bones perked up.

"No. Tell me. What happen?" he replied belligerently.

The shopkeeper's manner was blunt. "Their courier quit."

"Just like that?" The customer's eyebrows popped above the rim of his eyeglasses.

"Yes, just like that. The Plokhoys very angry." He began gesturing wildly. "The mafia look for guy who call himself Grim Reaper. He is responsible for courier quitting."

I gasped. In an instinctual defensive maneuver, I brought the open magazine up, just below my eye sockets, to cover my face bones.

The customer's eyes widened. "Oh?"

The shopkeeper rested his big, hairy forearm on the counter and took another puff of his cheap cigar. The smoke swirled between the two men. He leaned forward, tapped the foot of the cigar to shed the ashes, and looked the customer in the eye. "The mafia put a hit on this Reaper."

My knuckle bones went whiter.

"A hit?"

"Yes, a marriage hit."

"I get shivers," said the customer in his thick Russian accent.

"Heh, me too. When they find this Reaper, they gonna tie him down."

My breaths burst in and out, and a wave of chills overcame my bones.

"They gonna slap him."

My knee bones buckled.

"Then they gonna marry him off to the rudest, most demanding Russian woman in the Plokhoy agency."

I let out a yelp.

"Oh-oh, glad I'm not Reaper."

"Ha, me too. Bad, very bad for this Reaper." The shopkeeper shook his bald head.

Eye sockets wide as bone China dinner plates, I backed away inch by inch, still holding the unfolded magazine over my face bones.

Once I reached the door, my spine knocked into a bell on a string, jingling it.

The shopkeeper turned. He yelled out with an angry first in the air, "Hey, you! You pay for magazine," then charged after me. "Rubles! Rubles!"

I dropped the magazine, bolted out the door, and fled Russia, vowing never to return except to collect souls who were already dead, and who couldn't be forced to marry a very unfortunate reaper.

14

Nothing felt better than returning to headquarters. The Russian mafia couldn't touch me at the edge of the cosmos. I sprang up the spiral staircase, thrilled to be done with the chaos of the past several days. A heavy burden had been lifted, leaving me weightless as a goose feather.

Sighing, I let my finger bones glide against the banister. Lately, I'd clenched my teeth far too many days and grimaced far too many nights. But all this tension had released from my shoulder bones, and gratitude took over. I felt like a skeleton kite, hovering in midair over a grassy park on a warm summer day.

I shook myself, tickled by my recent achievements.

A skilled reaper never lost a soul, in this case, Jimmy's soul. Maintaining my clean track record, I'd keep my job. No more frightening thoughts of retirement. I wouldn't lose my identity so closely tied to my career or feel purposeless as I coasted in the in-between realm with nothing to do. No, I still boasted admirable spryness, and remained as alert and vigilant as a five-hundred-year-old.

And, solely due to my painstaking efforts, Jimmy was safe from the Russian mafia and an accidental life of crime. I smiled to myself and puffed out my rib cage.

I not only found his soul—I *saved* his soul.

Ha, I truly deserved the Employee of the Year award. I was a hero, a Super Reaper.

Amid my gloating, I reached the top of the stairs across from the offices. Death would be overjoyed to find out about my exhaustive snooping—and ultimate solving—of this highly bizarre predicament. I'd regain my professional integrity and still be a star. He'd celebrate with me.

Dry wiping my hand bones, I pulled open the glass door and sauntered in, my skull high and my chin bone out. Praises would surely come my way. After all, I'd just solved one half of a very big problem.

The other half puzzled me: how did Jimmy get on my list?

Stew waltzed past, carrying a silver tray of petit fours like a classy five-star restaurant's overzealous waiter. "Reaper, my favorite colleague. Help yourself to my latest delicacies."

I peeped down at the collection of iced, pastel yellow and pink cakes with delicate roses in the center. "Mm. Looks too good to eat."

"Nonsense. I baked them just so they *can* be eaten," he replied with an ear-to-ear grin.

What a charmer. "If you insist." I leaned down and picked up a few petit fours, then gobbled them up. "Delish, Stew. Just the right level of sweet and incredibly tender. Do I taste a hint of almond paste?"

"Nothing escapes you, huh? Almond paste, indeed. I knew you'd love them. Now, I've got to unload these fancy cakes on the rest of my favorite employees."

"You just love baking, don't you?"

"What can I say? I exist to bake."

He zipped off like a snowshoe hare fleeing danger. The little guy mystified me.

Death's door stood ajar—meaning he was in. I had a mind to jump up and down, but refrained for professional decorum. Leaving his office slightly open was the boss's way of letting the staff know he welcomed discussions about any work-related issues or suggestions to elevate the afterlife experience for the minute-by-minute stream of souls.

My duty was to inform him of the misadventures of the preceding days. With the situation ending on a high note, I had nothing to fear.

I knocked, clearing my throat.

"Yes?"

"Boss, it's me, Reaper."

He grunted and rolled his eyes. "You lose another soul, Reaper?"

Death hadn't forgotten. I gulped. This might be more challenging than I expected.

"Actually," I said, sliding through the opening, "I have better news."

He stopped fidgeting with his paperwork and glanced up at me. Cautiously, he said, "I'm listening."

I sat in the chair opposite his massive oak desk and took a deep breath. "See, boss, Jimmy's soul was never lost."

He arched his bushy eyebrow. "Is that so?"

"Jimmy's soul is still in his very much alive body."

Death leaned back with a huff, causing his executive swivel chair to squeak, and crossed his mighty arms over his equally enormous chest. "How can that be, Reaper? You going blind, too? I saw his soul on my computer clear as day. Now, listen, I've been considering offering you an early retirement package, you know, with severance pay and perks, like—"

My mouth went dry, and my empty stomach tightened.

As he rolled out the perks of retirement, I brought my hand bones up in front of myself and shook my skull. "No, no, boss," I interrupted. "Jimmy is alive. A-L-I-V-E."

Spelling it out for an imposing boss came out as desperate, but what else could I do to help him understand the gravity of the situation?

He froze, not twitching a muscle as he stared at me with his dark, penetrating gaze. I shifted in my seat, not knowing where to look. Maybe he'd found it offensive that I'd spelled out the pivotal word—the word that flipped the situation on its head. I hunched over in the chair, trying to make my skeleton as small as possible. Avoiding injury was highly advisable when dealing with a boss vexed beyond measure.

"How can you collect a soul if the body hasn't expired?" he asked, wide-eyed.

"I can't. That's the thing." I scooted to the edge of the seat. "See, Jimmy faked his own death and fled to Eastern Europe." I explained in rapid sequence, trying to get the words out before Death forced a severance package on me and ended my dream career.

I told him about the orange pants on the beach, the abandoned fishing boat, and Anne. The story went on as I described in detail how Jimmy had unwittingly ended up smuggling for the Russian mafia, the Plokhoy Bridal Agency's involvement, and his voluntary return to the States.

Death's eyes popped, and his jaw dropped. He didn't utter a word for a full minute.

"But...but, he was on the schedule." The boss didn't seem too sure of himself now.

I touched the back of my neck bone, flummoxed as he was. "Something's not right." My gaze shifted to a corner of the ceiling, then returned. "How'd he get on your schedule if you didn't put him there?"

"I-I don't know." Death shrugged repeatedly, and began fumbling with the loose papers strewn across his desk. "I've got to check it out. I'll compare my notes. I keep a paper schedule in my locked desk, which I refer to, then input those dates of death on my computer."

"So, essentially, you retain two records: one paper and one digital."

"Yes, that's right." The boss unlocked his desk drawer and dove into the paperwork. He pulled out a sheet with numerous pencil markings of scribbles, numbers, and a few doodles. Death had been around for ages, and I understood how he still relied on the traditional way of performing certain tasks. Paper was always a useful backup. Things could get tricky when relying on technology alone.

His dark eyes darted back and forth across the page. He rubbed his stubble chin. Then he brought the sheet closer to his face, as if to examine it more closely.

"This is strange."

I couldn't tolerate the anticipation. "What? What?"

"I never scheduled Jimmy Muffet's death."

I recoiled.

The boss showed me his paper schedule and pointed. "See? Right there."

Clear as plastic wrap, his soul was *not* listed for pickup at 20:01:36 in the West Bluff Picnic Area. In fact, his name didn't appear at all for that day.

A light rap sounded at the door. "Care for coffee cake?" a wee voice asked. "Moist, with cinnamon-streusel topping!"

"Not now, Stew," Death replied. "We're busy."

"Okay, but if you change your mind, it's in the break room. Toodaloo!"

The little spirit guide disappeared. What an angel, always looking out for the staff's well-being.

I returned my attention to the new details emerging in this case, which grew increasingly bizarre by the second. "So, your digital schedule shows his pickup, but your original paper notes don't?"

"Seems to be the case," Death replied, red in the face.

I leaned forward, my eye sockets bulging like moisture behind a wall, and whispered, "Boss, someone's hacked into your computer!"

We sat without a word.

Death finally broke the silence. "But why?"

I leaned back against the chair, my jawbone pursed, steeped in thought. "Technically, if you don't schedule a death, that individual lives forever."

"You're right, Reaper. Whoever hacked into my computer records intended for Jimmy to live indefinitely—because I never schedule a death twice."

My mind raced, returning to the recent events that unfolded in Moscow. Then it clicked.

"If Jimmy Muffet lived forever," I said, "the Russian mafia would have eternal access to a reliable, yet stupid, courier. They'd never have to hunt for another numskull again!"

"Reaper," Death said firmly, "you've got a point. Somebody gained access to my computer just long enough to alter the record." He pulled his broad shoulders back and narrowed his gaze. "We've got a traitor in the office. But who?"

"I know exactly who the traitor is."

15

The sounds of laughter ricocheted throughout the office. My rib cage tightened. I intended to express my displeasure at its source. My empty insides roiling, I stomped toward the hoots and hollers and rambunctious noise coming from the break room.

"Every day at the office is a party because of Stew!" It was Larry's squeaky voice.

A bubbly female, sounding like Cassandra, added, "Stew makes even work delicious." Despite being several steps away from the break room, my bones heated up.

Moe replied gruffly, "Not to mention his strawberry tarts. Yum!"

Ha—surprising that the grumpy, old spirit guide complimented anyone at all.

My insides churned like a spitting, fiery lava lake. How dare my colleagues enjoy a good time when a traitor was on the loose? That very traitor was among them, cavorting and acting silly in their company without them realizing it. My face bones flushed red.

Within seconds, I stormed into the break room, my fist bones on my hip bones, and my leg bones in a wide stance. I stood like a towering giant with steam pouring out of my ear bones and nasal cavity.

Cassandra glanced at me, her eyes full of mirth, and popped sliced apple pieces topped with gooey baked brie into her laughing mouth. "Reaper, you look way too grim." She handed me an apple slice. "Here, try Stew's baked brie. It'll put a smile on your face."

I didn't twitch a bone.

"Or perhaps a slice of pear?" she asked innocently.

"Maybe he needs something savory," Moe told her in a rough tone. He picked up two wooden skewers full of artichokes, meats, marinated cheeses, tomatoes, olives, green roasted peppers, and tortellini. "Here, Reaper, you need a couple of Stew's antipasto skewers." The grumpy spirit guide poked me in the rib cage with their pointy ends.

I flinched, only a little.

Then Larry offered me Stew's authentic guacamole dip. I lost it.

"Larry! Don't you play nice with me," I roared, my nasal cavity emitting smoke like a barbecue grill with too much burnt food residue.

The spirit guide dropped the plate of guacamole chips, his hands trembling.

"I know what you've been up to," I growled.

Larry jerked his head back. Panic filled his eyes. I'd nabbed him, and he knew it.

I pointed my long finger bone at him. "It was you all along, wasn't it?"

Cassandra and Moe had stopped munching their apples and antipasto to gawk up at me.

"Wh-what are you talking about, Reaper?" Larry asked, his voice and body shaking. Spirit guides with a guilty conscience always shuddered visibly.

"You messed with Death's schedule."

His eyes popped. Beads of sweat slid down his temples. He couldn't even conceal his horrifying betrayal.

"You hacked into the boss's computer when he wasn't there," I said.

Larry shook his head. "N-no, I didn't."

"Of course you did." I outlined his alleged actions in detail, in case he forgot. "You snuck in when the boss wasn't around. In that brief minute—that's all it took—you accessed his computer, added Jimmy Muffet's date and time and place of death. Then, when Death returned, he sent the schedule to my phone, as he usually did, but without realizing the schedule had been altered!"

A burst of hot air shot out through my nasal cavity. "You double-crosser," I went on, "you sent me on a wild soul chase. I was almost married off!"

Larry sat speechless, still gawking at me with his mouth dropped nearly to the tile floor.

Then he began to slowly shake his head, as if in disbelief. "No, no, Reaper. It wasn't me. I swear. I—"

"I know *why* you did it too." I glared at him. "You're trying to sabotage my chances of winning the Employee of the Year award, aren't you! You can't stand that I'll win again. What a sore loser." I crossed my arm bones across my rib cage and tapped my feet bones rapidly. "You know we're both vying for the award. You also know I have the best chances of winning. Disgruntled as you are, you—"

Larry threw his turnip-red face into his hands and bawled uncontrollably.

Cassandra put her arm around his shoulder and whispered, "Hush, hush."

Moe, with raised, bushy eyebrows, kept glancing back and forth between Larry and me, as if watching a boxing match in the ring and unsure who to root for.

Just then, Stew rushed into the break room. The petite spirit guide had the gall to stand between Larry and me with his arms out. "Entities, entities, please. Gentle entities don't fight."

I jerked my skull back, as Larry sobbed louder.

"You're friends, colleagues, remember? Awards aren't everything. But friendship is." The diminutive spirit guide's tone was calm, almost pacifying.

This was déjà vu. I'd been through this before. Sweet-talking Stew always came to the rescue. But I couldn't disregard a spirit guide who'd perfected croquembouche. No one built a cream puff tower in a caramel cage without angelic powers.

I shook my skull, feeling the urge to withdraw. The initial fire that fueled me waned to a flicker—for the moment. It was no use accusing someone who repeatedly denied their wrongdoings. I backed off.

Cassandra, Larry, and Stew silently watched me leave. Moe still gawked at me with his mouth open, but with a slight frown, as if disappointed he didn't get to see the knockout he'd anticipated.

Before I exited the break room, I spun around at the doorway and warned, "Larry, you better prepare yourself. The Grim Reaper will win the Employee of the Year award this year too. Humph!" I lifted my chin bone into the air and strutted off.

I ignored hearing Cassandra comforting Larry with soothing words.

Still fuming, I returned to my cubicle. I cursed under my breath, stomping around, and pounding my fist bone on my desk. The metal paperclips jiggled, producing a light, cheery jingle.

"Oh, shush," I said to them with a scowl.

I couldn't think clearly. All I knew was that Larry was the traitor. I'd suspected him all along. He was the only colleague who had a motive: to destroy a professional rival and take home the spoils. By messing with my list and making me look incompetent, he increased his chances of winning the popular vote and the award itself—the award I deserved.

How some spirit guides stooped so low never failed to surprise me.

16

A couple days later, I noshed on a coconut pecan tart, although my mind was focused not on the sweet, crunchy filling but elsewhere—like beyond the next, next world. I didn't feel completely present in the break room, though my physical skeleton literally was.

As I zoned out, losing track of time, Stew strolled in.

His sunny presence disturbed my dark reflections of the upsetting incident a few days ago. He was like a welcome ray of light in a soulless room. "Hey, Reaper, my favorite colleague," he said, greeting me in his high-spirited tone. "Hope you're enjoying the tarts."

"Hm? Oh, um, yeah, they're great, really delish. You can do no wrong, Stew. We're glad to have someone like you in the office, always looking after us, making sure we're fed and happy." I gave him a quarter-smile. It was all I could muster, having been drained by the big fight with Larry.

"Aw," he said, his blushing face as coy as a cherub's. "Glad you like them. They didn't take long to whip up, just a few hours beginning at three o'clock in the morning."

I jerked back my skull. He woke up at three o'clock? "You're really dedicated."

"Every single one of my wonderful colleagues deserves it." He set a large sheet cake on the counter. "Help yourself. Freshly made, too, while the tarts were in the oven."

I glanced over. In green frosting, surrounded by rainbow sprinkles, it read, "Colleagues are Family."

"Thanks, Stew. I will."

"I'll be baking you a celebration sheet cake when you win the Employee of the Year award." He gestured expansively. "It'll be written with 'Congratulations' in big letters and topped with sugar skull bones."

"Sounds awesome."

I sat clicking my jawbone, disconnected from my surroundings, despite Stew being here and lending the place much-needed cheer. I stared at the blank wall as Stew wiped his hands on a towel.

He approached, still cleaning his hands. "It's a shame Larry proved to be the traitor." Stew's eyes seemed saddened. It's the first time I'd seen him glum.

Nibbling what was left of the tart, I looked at him briefly. "Yeah." I long sigh escaped my jawbone. Larry, humph. Who'd have thought he, of all spirit guides, could resort to deceit? A mix of difficult emotions riddled me to the bone.

I'd known Larry a long time, centuries. My empty insides sank to the bottom of my bones. A heaviness overcame me. We'd kept our distance from each other since the big blow-out. I almost felt the need to inflict pain on myself as penance. But he'd done wrong—not me.

"Traitors are horrible. They ought to be banished into limbo, where they'd do their time very uncomfortably." Stew shot me a glance that made my bones shudder.

"Can't trust a double-dealer," he said, continuing his tirade. "How can you work with someone knowing they're a backstabber? They don't deserve to win an award as highly esteemed as the Employee of the Year. If they did, it'd be ridiculous, as ridiculous as asking a fiancé to wear an orange wedding dress."

I coughed, spitting out the coconut pecan tart.

Dropping the tart like a hot potato, I turned to Stew. "How do you know about the orange wedding dress?"

He blinked rapidly. His neck flushed as he babbled. "Wh-what? I-I don't know." He stumbled over his words, breaking eye contact. "Orange wedding dresses are, um, common."

"No, they're not," I said with furrowed brow bones. "Asking a fiancé to wear an orange wedding dress isn't something you hear every day, if ever. You know something."

He spoke a stream of nonsense, apologizing profusely in between, before releasing a strangled-sounding laugh.

"He-he, well, you know, we spirit guides know everything."

He glanced around, pulling at his collar. "It's getting hot in here. Can we open a window?"

My nasal cavity flared. "There are no windows in the break room."

I rose from my chair. The legs screeched like nails on a chalkboard as they scraped against the tile floor.

Stew looked up at me, his tiny body quivering beneath the shadow of my towering skeleton.

"No, spirit guides don't know everything," I said, rolling up my cloak sleeves. "Rookie spirit guides aren't given full access to the earthly realm. It's impossible for a newbie to have information like that, unless—"

His lips trembling, he shielded his face while backing away inch by inch.

I strode to the counter and grabbed his sheet cake. "This looks lovely. The frosting, perhaps smooth, creamy vanilla buttercream?"

He let out a sigh and smiled. "Why, yes, buttercream. I-I know everyone in the office loves vanilla. I only aim to please, he-he!"

I glanced down at the decorations. "Beautiful flowers. So delicately hued and perfectly piped. I bet the inside tastes as good as the outside looks."

Stew's shoulders relaxed. He wiped his sweaty forehead with the back of his hand. "Oh, thank goodness. Yes, I hope so. I put a lot of effort into it."

Carrying the sheet cake, I casually walked over to the corner of the break room. Stew's eyes followed my every move. Standing over the big, blue trash bin, I asked in a leisurely tone, "How'd you like this sumptuous sheet cake, fine as it is, to meet the bottom of the garbage can?"

I ended with a smile. Stew's pupils dilated. He began hyperventilating, waving his palms in front of himself. "No, no, please don't."

I lowered the cake a few inches downward. In a firm tone, I demanded, "Spill the beans or this cake hits the trash."

He stood silent, his eyes darting side to side, clearly not knowing what to do.

He refused to respond, so I lowered the cake farther, this time halfway into the garbage can. "The only thing that'll eat this is the bottom of the trash receptacle."

Stew sweated profusely. He bit his lips and scraped his hand over his bald head.

"It's going...going," I said.

"Okay, okay! I'll talk. Just don't throw my vanilla butter-cream frosted sheet cake away!"

I halted all movement.

Stew sighed, then sat on a chair, his short legs dangling without touching the floor. Gazing downward, his face became dark. The stubble on his chin and the deep lines under his now-sunken eyes grew pronounced. He no longer looked like sweet, little Stew.

I gulped, staring at his transformation.

Suddenly, he broke out in a Russian accent: "It is the fault of Madame Katerina."

I stepped back. Madame Katerina? Her name rang a bell, but I couldn't place her. I scratched my skull. Seconds ticked away—until it struck me.

She was the Russian mafia's personal medium, the woman Jimmy had been consulting before he went missing. She'd connected me with Duplicity of the Plokhoy Bridal Agency! Our first and only phone call replayed in my mind.

"Madame Katerina and I, we remain in contact. She tell me everything." Stew's five o'clock shadow seemed to appear out of nowhere. It aged him right before my eye sockets.

But Stew's claim checked out. Only psychic mediums had access to both the earthly and otherworldly realms. Madame Katerina was the bridge between the earthly sphere and the next world. She'd been Stew's earthly contact for sinister purposes.

"Who contacted Madame Katerina?" I asked. I had my hunches, but needed to clarify.

"It was brother and sister team. In Moscow," Stew replied in his thick Russian accent. His tone of voice was no longer bright and chipper but deep and rough. What a change, like night and day, this world and the next. "They run bridal agency."

The Plokhoys! I knew it. Energy zipped through my bones. "Why did they contact Madame Katerina?"

"They need reliable courier," Stew said matter-of-factly. "They too lazy to replace couriers every few months. So, they arrange to have a courier who lives and works forever."

I gasped. That's why Stew hacked into Death's computer scheduling system—to make it look like Jimmy had passed. That way, the boss wouldn't schedule his death ever again, ensuring the mafia made good on their wish to recruit a bonehead who'd literally smuggle for them into eternity!"

It all made sense now. The Russian mafia had their in-house medium, Madame Katerina, contact Stew, an unscrupulous spirit guide willing to do their dirty work in the afterlife. Stew applied for the spirit guide position at headquarters to execute this brazen scheme. He would've gotten away with it if it weren't for Jimmy's obsession with orange—specifically, an orange wedding dress!

The break room seemed to spin. Dizzy, I nearly dropped the sheet cake. Stew ran under me and caught the cake slipping out of my hand bones. Then he bolted out of the break room.

"Stop!" I yelled, quickly returning to my senses. But he'd grabbed his backpack and, with the cake, sped off.

I ran out of the break room after him. Moe moseyed on by, calm and dull as pumpernickel.

"Moe, call security," I said, with an air of urgency. "And get Death, quick!"

"Oh, okay, Reaper," he mumbled, unphased, and lumbered on.

I had no time to see if the old spirit guide called for the boss. I scrambled in the direction Stew had fled. But he'd vanished, out of sight. I stood at the entrance to the office, scratching my skull and looking left and right—but to no avail. Stew had escaped.

Just then, Death arrived. "What's going on?"

"Boss, am I glad to see you. I have no time to explain. Stew, he's the traitor!"

"What? Sweet Stew? Reaper, you losin' your marbles, getting confused by too much sugar?"

"I can't explain right now. But he admitted everything."

My eye sockets scanned my immediate environment. That's when a trail of lacy, white doilies on the carpeting grabbed my attention. I held both sides of my skull. Pointing, I screamed, "Follow the doilies!"

Death, Moe, and I closely followed the trail of white doilies, which likely had fallen, one by one, out of Stew's backpack as he attempted to flee. We reached the lobby, all three of us panting like old-timers.

Through heavy puffs of breath that made his gray whiskers flap, Moe said, "I can't go any farther. Both of you, go on. Save yourselves."

I rolled my eye sockets. Moe, the cantankerous drama king.

Then, through the glass door, I spotted a wee figure outside in the lot, holding a cake three times bigger than his body.

"There he is!"

Security rushed from behind us, down the front steps and into the lot, where they tackled Stew. The disgraced spirit guide fell face-first into his sheet cake, giving him a buttercream frosting mustache and eyebrows.

The two brawny security guides shackled him as Death and I reached the scene.

With his beady eyes narrowed and a tight-lipped frown, Stew looked as mean as an average number. Security cuffed him, arms behind his back, and hauled him away, as he wriggled. "I'd have gotten away with it," he growled, "if it weren't for you meddling, Reaper!"

Death gave him one look, assessing the whole situation, and shouted, "Stew, you're fired."

Stew spat at the ground. "Pohhui."

The boss turned to me and asked, "What did he say?"

"To put it mildly, he doesn't care."

17

Death grunted and cursed under his breath as we ascended the spiral staircase back to the office. "I can't believe this Jimmy Muffet put my staff through this nonsense." His lips twisted into an ugly curl.

On our way up, he slammed his mighty fist against the rail several times. I jumped in my bones at every whack-a-mole-like pounding. Someone as towering and angry as Death could do significant damage when irked.

We reached the top of the stairs and navigated toward Death's door, the boss's dusky face visibly red and growing redder by the second. He criticized the situation nonstop through clenched teeth. Finally, he plonked into his executive swivel chair with a resounding thump. I scurried into the seat across.

He began working at his computer, typing keys in quick succession. His posture tense, he continuously slammed glass jars of paperclips and threw USB chargers against the wall.

"Boss, are you okay?" I asked. "I realize we just had to call security to take care of an explosive situation, but you ought to be glad you ousted a rogue spirit guide. By the sound of things, you seem vexed."

Consumed by his work, the boss didn't face me but focused intensely on the computer screen.

"Listen, Reaper," he said. "This Jimmy Muffet put us in a bad position, screwing us over. I'm so mad, I'm already scheduling his death for within the next six months—and this time, there'll be no mistake. I'll give him a fatal illness that'll put him on the fast track to an untimely demise. He earned it for putting my team through agony. No one messes with Death." He turned away from the computer screen and looked at me. "What d'you think, lung cancer, advanced heart disease, or organ failure?"

I sat speechless. Death appeared utterly serious.

"Uh," I said, stalling and darting my gaze, unsure where to look. In the minute of silence that followed, it was clear he waited for an answer. Death wasn't joking.

"Boss, it wasn't Jimmy's fault," I spurted out, leaning across his desk. "He's not the sharpest tool in the shed. He didn't know what he was getting himself into." With an Italian shrug, I pointed out, "Who knew the neighborhood's psychic medium had ties with the Russian mafia?"

Defending Jimmy, I felt a bit embarrassed for him. Who else but him would believe a box of chocolate weighed the equivalent of a large goat?

I sighed and sat back. "The poor guy deserves a break. If you met his wife, you'd understand. He was just looking for love in all the wrong places." In a somber tone, I pleaded. "Jimmy ought to be pardoned."

Death met my gaze and held it for a few uncertain seconds. He seemed to study me, as if amused that I could fight for such a simpleton. At last, he exhaled. "Fine, Reaper. You seem to know him better than I. After all, you dealt with him personally. I'll consider your recommendation." He stared off into the distance for a minute, then returned to the conversation. "It's settled. I'll pardon him, Reaper. That's one less soul to deal with today." He turned and resumed typing, but at a calmer pace.

"Thanks, boss," I said with a crisp nod. "He's not a bad guy, just a little lost."

I stood up, exited, and returned to my desk.

I kept in touch with Jimmy for a short while after that fiasco. He'd come out of hiding in the Bay Area and relocated south to Orange County, a nice touristy area with lots of beaches, theme parks, and world-class resorts. He'd made a new life for himself in the picturesque, coastal parts of southern California. Though, sadly, he was in the midst of a divorce battle with Anne and terribly lonely.

Trying to offer solace, I advised him to buy tickets to the Orange Bowl. It was right up his alley. Hanging out at one of the most prestigious college football bowl games, he'd surely meet his type of gal.

"Smile at the nice girl sitting next to you in the stands," I told him over the phone. "Join the fab pre-game parties. Be sure to wear team apparel to blend in with fellow fans. Most of all, have fun with the whole experience."

He let me know that, once he found someone, he'd invite me to his wedding.

"I wouldn't miss it for the afterworld," I said.

The office remained quiet in the days after Death fired Stew. No more raucous laughter echoing from the break room or spirited team luncheons, where we sat down together and feasted on blooming quesadilla rings. Lunches returned to uneventful early afternoons, bland as supermarket white bread.

Normal, everyday interactions with my colleagues seemed awkward, stilted, and lacking. Without mouthwatering pesto pinwheels and colorful fruit platters to greet and excite us each day, it was hardly surprising that things didn't seem like they used to.

Cassandra, especially, missed Stew. One day, when I walked into the break room, she sat munching on boxed salted crackers, dry as the Arizona desert, when I walked in. Her misty eyes stared vacantly. "You know, Reaper, this cracker sure would taste better with Stew's homemade baked camembert."

I sat down next to her and leaned in. "Yeah, or maybe his famous brie." I shook my skull. "What a guy."

The countertop looked bare, without trays of grilled fruit kabobs and vanilla-honey dips, tiered stands of chocolate cake donuts, and piles of sandwiches stuffed with delicious fillings.

"There'll never be another Stew," she cried out, her voice breaking. "I never even got to tell him how inspiring his charcuterie boards were." She sniffled, staring down at her hands.

I offered her a tissue.

"Thanks, Reaper." She dabbed her puffy face. "I think I'll go now." She trudged off to her cubicle, wiping away tears.

Just then, Larry sauntered in. My face bones grew paler, and my posture slumped.

He nodded briefly at me, then busied himself at the coffee machine.

I gave him repeated glances, feeling compelled to break the silence, yet holding myself back. A heaviness filled my rib cage.

We hadn't spoken in days. Even courteous hellos had fallen by the wayside. I sat quietly fidgeting with the folds of my cloak, as he prepared his cup of coffee with his back turned to me.

I dropped my skull into my hand bones. How could I let this go on? We'd been colleagues—friends—for a long time. I felt the strong desire to amend my actions and offer a redress for my erroneous accusations. I'd been self-critical ever since the real traitor had been identified, leaving me with a mild case of anxiety around Larry.

As the stream of coffee poured into his cup, bubbling and splattering, I made up my mind. I'd tap into my latent humility and bring myself to say the five-letter word: *sorry*. It didn't come easily to a reaper. I couldn't recall the last time I'd apologized to anyone. But Larry's comradeship meant a lot to me.

I cleared my throat. "Ah, Larry?"

He turned his head. "Yeah, Reaper?"

"Listen, I—"

"Yeah?" He rushed toward me, leaning forward, with his white foam cup.

"Uh, I just need a second." I coughed, then straightened my spine. Inhaling deeply, I started. "Larry, we're colleagues. We've been at this afterlife game for eons. And together. I-I—"

I choked up again. It took a few seconds to collect myself. But Larry's soft, brown eyes sparkled as he looked into
my eye sockets, paying rapt attention.

"I want to apologize for blaming you." I felt a wave of relief. I'd said it. I just didn't know if my apology would make
a difference. After all, I'd hurled angry accusations at him
for no good reason.

But I did a double take when he said, with a wave of his
hand, "Aww, Reaper, you don't need to apologize. It was
only—"

I looked incredulously into his forgiving face, then
grabbed him by the arm. "No, really, Larry. I hope you accept my apology for letting a trivial award come between
our longtime fellowship, one that I respect and that means
the afterworld to me. Every one of my colleagues is important in my book. I'm truly sorry I laid blame on you, an
innocent spirit guide who never did anybody in the afterworld wrong."

His stared at me, wide-eyed. I looked down, realizing
my tight grip probably made him uncomfortable. I let go
and stepped back, extending my hand bone. "Larry, will
you accept my apology?"

He smiled big, shoved my hand bone away, and said,
"Come here, Reaper. Of course, I accept your apology." He
pulled me in and gave me a giant bear hug.

A warm, fuzzy feeling filled my empty insides. It was
great to be comrades again.

18

Nominations for the Employee of the Year award were underway. I hustled during the last few days of the nomination period, drumming up votes in my favor.

I handed out nomination forms to spirit guides, angles, and cherubs who couldn't write a complete grammatical sentence. With my name, department, and job title pre-populated, all they had to do was fill out the very achievements that made me deserving of this award. If they were up for it, they could also write in how my actions positively impacted the afterlife organization as a whole.

For those savvy with the written word, I encouraged them to write nomination letters to the review committee. Letters, being lengthier, described the relationships I held with my colleagues as well as my measurable impacts. Specific examples of my top-notch skills were always appreciated.

First stop: the cherubs hanging out in the office court-yard. Under a canopy of a baby blue sky, I inhaled the refreshing air, as pure as the colleagues I was about to address.

"Freddie, your nomination helps foster a positive work environment," I said to the chubby cherub with tousled brown hair, handing him an anonymous nomination form. "It's important everyone is included, including Sammy and Annalise." I gave him a wink. "Pass the word along to the rest of the cherubs."

He dropped his gaze down at me lazily from his perch in the puffy white clouds, laid his dimpled chin on his fleshy palm, and sighed through his rosy, parted lips.

I took that as a yes, gave him a thumbs bone up, and moved on.

A group of angels crowded in the lower-level cafeteria. My chin bone held high, I strode up to them. "Angels, I want to thank you in advance for your support of the next employee of the year, *moi*. I'd be tickled white if you'd recognize my efforts in your nominations: initiative, innovation in the collections process, achieving targets consistently, and regular attendance. You've never heard me call in sick!"

The angels looked at me, yawned, and flapped their immense, feathery white wings.

Another clear indication of support. I thrust out my rib cage, in complete control. With a cocky smile, I continued my hustle.

Back in the office, Cassandra sat at her desk, her frizzy, brunette hair cascading down her shoulders, as she knitted her brows and scribbled away at paperwork.

I leaned over her cubicle wall and flashed her a thousand-watt grin. "Psst. If you need help with nomination context, I'm your guy."

She looked up, her eyebrows arching. "Reaper! I'm writing your nomination letter as we speak," she said in her customary chipper tone. Her words were music to my ear bones. I surveyed her letter, pleased.

"My preferred full name is Grim Reaper," I said, pointing to the line where she'd simply written "Reaper."

"Oh, sorry about that." Cassandra quickly added "Grim."

"My employee identification number is the cosmic number three followed by a googol of zeros."

"Got it. Thanks."

Things proceeded swimmingly. I bid the cheerful spirit guide adieu and rubbed my hand bones, feeling a rush of positive energy pulse through my skeleton.

Larry strolled past. We exchanged a few pleasantries, with me saying, "Larry, may the best entity win." He gave me a wistful, almost sad expression. I patted him on the shoulder as he whizzed away.

Feeling relaxed and up for anything, I approached the next spirit guide on my agenda. His characteristically grumpy demeanor altered my swooning state—just a tad.

"Moe, how are ya today?" I asked, slapping him on his hunched back.

The old spirit guide hurled forward from the slap, teetering slightly on his feet. Taken aback my own strength, I cleared my throat and said, "Um, my dignified colleague, delivering exemplary customer service, unmatched in all of eternity—"

Moe pulled his eyebrows to the bridge of his nose. He huffed, flapping his long, gray whiskers.

"I'm just here to remind you of my service to the afterlife enterprise and all that qualifies me to win the award in the next couple days."

With a sideways glance, he grunted and rolled his eyes.

"Now, it's important to use words that describe me in particular, like 'best' and 'inspiring.' Or, better yet, 'outstanding' and 'excellent,' and don't forget 'talented'!"

He pursed his thin lips and tilted his head. I upped my game.

"Moe, we enjoy a special eternal connection. We've worked together endlessly to achieve the goals of bringing souls safely to the other side and giving them a dandy afterworld experience: me rowing souls over the river, and you guiding them from the banks of eternity to the brilliant haven of the next world." My fist bones on my hip bones, I bookended my flattery. "We're like peanut butter and jelly—two irresistible condiments that simply go well together."

Eyeing me, he stroked his gray beard, then shuffled around his desk looking busy.

Clearly, I'd made my impact. Leaving with a smile, I reminded the curmudgeonly spirit guide, "And remember to mention my sunshiny personality traits in your nomination letter!"

I returned to my desk to begin writing my own email to nominate myself in a self-promotion campaign. After all, I certainly merited the Employee of the Year award, and who better knew the extent of my lasting contributions? Combined with nomination forms and letters from my colleagues, the award review committee would receive numerous perspectives and make the most informed decision.

In short, the award was mine.

I'd tell them about improving the soul retention rate by 1.8 percent and resolving a recent dispute about a supposedly missing soul. Despite having a full queue, I made time and effort to find *and* save his soul. That alone was award-worthy of perhaps a dozen awards. Furthermore, my productivity continued to be exemplary, and I always pitched in on team projects, no matter how trivial or consequential. However, since we dealt in the steady business of souls, everything held significance in the afterworld.

A place in the Afterlife Headquarters' Hall of Fame called my name. I stared off dreamily.

I began typing, when I recalled several more of my past year's accomplishments.

Could I fit them all in one email? My eye sockets veered off to the corner of the office, looking for answers. I shook my head. There were just too many notable successes to list. Surely, it was a good problem to have. I mean, who else on the team contributed as much as I did?

I'd focus on generalizations to improve my chances.

I grew absorbed in penning my email:

Dear Nomination Committee:

I am writing this email to nominate the one and only Grim Reaper for this year's Employee of the Year award. Yes, that's yours truly.

As a diligent worker who serves the afterlife with unparalleled dedication, I am an incredibly valuable team member. This month alone, I collected five million souls and gave each and every one of them safe passage to the other side, our beautiful, glorious side.

I am a hard worker who is appreciated by my colleagues, whose nomination letters in praise of me you should be receiving shortly. I am among the most experienced team members, having served in my role for over seven hundred years—a mere blink of an eye in the scheme of things, but still worth mentioning.

As the Grim Reaper, I may boast of a grim manner; but, my true claim to fame is the friendly charm I deliver when interacting with souls, inspiring and motivating them to flee in the opposite direction. There is no question I am a worthwhile candidate for this prestigious award.

I go above and beyond—literally.

Sincerely,

Grim Reaper

I hit *Send*, and sat back with a confident smile.

19

The day arrived at last. I climbed over rows of knobby spirit guides' knees and pushed through sweeping angels' wings, clamoring to take a seat in the front. Spirit guides from the far reaches of eternity, some whose faces I didn't even recognize, as well as angels and cherubs, all tightly packed the auditorium like military style rolled socks. The room buzzed with nonstop excitement.

Golden suspended auditorium lights shone on the empty stage, setting a suspenseful mood.

I settled in a plush red stadium rocker seat, reminiscent of movie theater chairs in the earthly sphere. I drummed my finger bones against the arm rest, rocking to and fro, trying to calm my bundle of nerves. My attention never veered from the stage, as I mentally rehearsed my acceptance speech over and over. Today would be one of the most gratifying experiences of all year.

Ten agonizing minutes later, the lights changed color, transitioning from a mesmerizing golden to a royal purple, pulsing and fading, as if to tease me. A dazzling light show had begun, poking fun at my intense desire to be on stage accepting my award. As the light show silently tormented me, the auditorium gradually hushed, with some attendees *oohing* and *aahing*.

Splendid Life, wearing a glittery blue sequined dress, strutted up to the podium and tapped the mic. "Good afternoon." She scanned the audience left to right. "What a crowd. I see a lot of familiar faces. It's great to be here with all of you for the 4.5 billionth employee recognition ceremony."

A few entities clapped softly. I simply gawked at my beautiful eternal crush, looking stunning on stage.

She cleared her throat. "I am Life, your master of ceremonies. Our presentation today will include singing of the afterlife anthem and music from the local angel rock band, opening remarks by Death, and the formal recognition of our Employee of the Year award recipient."

Angels in the back threw their feathered arms into the air, whistling and hooting.

From one corner of the auditorium, trumpets played. A winged vocalist from the angel choir began to sing, "Oh, say can you hear, the angels..."

I sat entranced by her harmonious song, while seeing photos of various afterlife staff at work, inspiring smiles, lending a helping hand, or offering guidance, splash on the big screen. Funny, I didn't see a single photo of me. I slumped and let my chin bone fall into my hand bone.

A few minutes later, the glorious music died down. Life returned to the podium. "Let's give a hand to the sensational angel vocalist!"

The audience clapped. I folded my arm bones across my rib cage and grunted, wondering where my photo was. Maybe whoever organized the ceremony forgot to include one. I sagged back in my seat.

"We enjoy immense success as we serve Earth, and today we review those accomplishments," Life said, her melodious voice exuding joy mixed with pride. "We've achieved so much in the earthly sphere, and have been blessed with another impactful year. Let's keep the Afterlife Headquarters' engine humming."

More hoots and hollers sounded from the audience. I tilted my skull back and looked up at the ceiling. Why couldn't they get on with it? The most important part would be me holding my award.

"We all work together in service to Earth, and we can't do this without the contributions of each and every one of you. It is my honor to recognize the hard work of hundreds of thousands of spirit guides and team members across the entire afterlife enterprise."

Life beamed. She glanced around, as if addressing each audience member personally. That was the magic of Life and what made her so deserving of my eternal adoration. She simply made it feel like she hand-crafted every creature, which she literally did.

"Now, I'll turn over the award ceremony to my nearest and dearest, Death." She clapped as the boss took to the stage like a savanna elephant charging ahead in full display of its strength.

I bit my knuckle bone. My knee bones bounced. Trying to stay still, I grabbed them with my hand bones, but my anticipation burst into full force. My skeleton began to visibly tremble. The angel sitting next to me laid a gentle hand on my shoulder bone. But her calming effort was in vain.

This was the moment, the moment I'd been waiting for all year. My alertness heightened.

Death began to speak, his voice sonorous. "We are gathered this afternoon to recognize the standard of excellence established by the Afterlife enterprise: a commitment to the welfare of souls, hard work, leadership, support of the afterlife mission, and achievement of the highest bar set in the cosmos."

I tapped my feet bones on the floor. The cherub sitting on the other side of me whispered, "Shh".

I shushed him back.

The boss continued. "Today I recognize the outstanding employee who exemplifies afterlife ideals and contributes to our standard of excellence, an individual who consistently exceeds expectations, and whose performance distinguishes them from their peers."

Butterflies flitted around my abdominal cavity. I grew dizzy. What if they forgot to display my photo onscreen because I lacked importance? Was I even considered an award candidate? Doubts plagued my restless mind. I couldn't control my sudden onslaught of worries. I began to fear the worst.

"Reaper, please take center stage," Death said, looking directly at me.

Then, just as spontaneously as the panic arose, it stopped.

I looked at the angel and cherub on either side of me, then pointed to myself. "Me?"

"Yes, you," the cherub said and pushed me out of my seat.

I ambled toward the stage, stumbling up the steps, pretending nothing awkward had just happened. The audience kept their eyes glued on me.

Despite the anticipation, the worries, the fears, my moment had come. The boss had only one reason to call me on stage—to give me my just reward.

I positioned myself under the golden light beam, my hand bones clasped in front of me. My skeleton began to sweat. I was the shining star.

Death glanced over at me and began to speak. His mouth appeared to move in slow motion, but I couldn't hear a word. Seized again by anticipation, I stood shaking in front of everyone.

"The employee of the year..." Death gestured his immense hand toward me. "...is Grim Reaper!"

I slapped my hand bones against my cheekbones, assailed by shock, satisfaction, and again more shock. Winning a prestigious award like this was astonishing, even though I deserved it one hundred percent. Reality and imagination were two different beasts, the former far more satisfying.

I basked in the glorious sensation of winning, then took a breath and pranced across the stage.

Death smiled, holding the golden trophy, as luminous as the blazing center of a galaxy. He extended the prize to me, and, with a nod, I accepted it.

The afterlife photographer snapped photos of Death and me holding each side of the trophy, me with my mega-watt smile and the boss with his dusky grin.

Unable to contain my smile, I stepped aside a few inches to let the boss speak.

"Reaper is an exemplary leader who enhances the delivery of souls," Death said to the audience. "He has single-handedly collected sixty-one million souls over the year and orchestrated their safe passages to the other side.

He has delivered outstanding results, never leaving a soul behind in limbo. Our very own Reaper is a brilliant and inspiring leader who thrives in his challenging role."

"Aw, thanks, boss," I said, twisting my skeleton coyly.

Death added, "We're glad he doesn't exceed performance targets and collect more souls than necessary, as that would mess me up pretty badly."

He gestured me toward the mic. "Say a few words, Reaper."

Rib cage thrust out, I took to the podium and looked out at the vast sea of faces. "Thank you for this honor. It's a great feeling to have my work recognized. This award is the validation I need to keep going." I held up the trophy high, shaking it triumphantly in the air.

I continued my acceptance speech with unstoppable fervor. "Winning this prestigious award is an unforgettable moment, one that will go down in afterlife history for generations to witness and know that even a lowly Reaper can ascend to the greatest heights. I—"

My gaze drifted to the front. At once, my chest cavity sank. There sat Larry, his watery eyes downcast, the corners of his lips in a frown, his body crumpled in his seat.

I grew unwell. My bottom jawbone quivered. I almost felt his poignant sadness mixed with disappointment. As I stood on stage, my attention remained transfixed on the forlorn spirit guide. Memories of our shared good times flooded my mind: the laughter, the corny jokes, the pats on the backbone. Growing dizzy under the spotlight, I couldn't take it.

Without even realizing, my speech took a one-eighty-degree turn. "Entities gathered here today, let me share with you what one special spirit guide once said to me: that awards aren't everything."

The audience began to murmur and shift in their seats.

"He's gone, but he's one spirit guide I'll never forget. Now I understand the meaning of his words. As I stand up here today, holding this precious award, I realize I don't need it to feel validated, to know my work is appreciated. Each one of you shows me that every day."

I cleared my throat. "But there's one entity who deserves this award more than I do, an entity who embodies the light and love of the afterworld, an entity who shows forgiveness, goodwill, and kindness, never saying a bad word even in the face of awful accusations."

The angels, cherubs, and spirit guides looked at each other with raised eyebrows.

"Larry, come on up here." I gestured at him with a wave.

The spirit guide, a quizzical expression on his face, stepped onto the stage.

"Larry, I'd like to bestow this Employee of the Year award on you, because you truly are the employee of the year." I handed the trophy to him with a smile.

He accepted the gleaming award, holding it in his chunky hands. "Aw shucks, thanks, Reaper," he said into the mic. "I never won anything before. This is awesome, just awesome."

He wiped away happy tears, posed proudly for the photographer, then hopped off the stage.

Life returned to the podium. "What a Reaper, never failing to surprise us. This concludes our award ceremony. Please join me in a round of applause. Thank you for your participation. You're invited to join the new awardee for food and drink in the Afterlife Headquarters Café."

20

Over the following weeks, the daily grind returned to normal. Every now and then someone would bring in a box of glazed donuts, and the staff would scramble for them. But still, it wasn't like walking into an onsite bakery anymore, where a smorgasbord of freshly baked delights greeted us every single day.

None of us would ever forget Stew. He was one of a kind, a spirit guide who'd lost his way but had managed to help us know who and what we valued.

One uneventful day, after transporting the souls on my list, I returned to headquarters. As I strolled toward my desk, I noticed an unusual, brightly colored item sitting on it.

Tilting my skull to the side, I quickened my pace. I reached for it, only to discover it was a sealed orange envelope. My feisty finger bones hastily opened it.

My eye sockets popped—it was a bright orange wedding invitation.

"Jimmy and Jennifer, together with their families, cordially invite you to attend their wedding." I glanced into the distance. "Hmm."

What a nice surprise. He'd finally found the right gal, someone who loved orange enough to send out solid orange wedding invitations.

I smiled to myself, admiring the tiny flowers and white calligraphy on the front.

Suddenly, I froze. How did someone from the earthly sphere deliver this invitation to the next realm? I stared at it with bewilderment.

Jimmy knew of only one person who bridged his world with the next: Madame Katerina.

I gulped.

The Russian mafia!

"Eek!"

Thank you for reading *The Soul Who (Almost) Got Away: A Grim Reaper Mystery Comedy Adventure.*
If you enjoyed this adventure, please share your thoughts in a review!

Books in the Grim Reaper Adventure series
A Morbid Obsession: A Grim Reaper Comedy Adventure
Crossing Over and Back: A Grim Reaper Comedy Adventure
A Holly Jolly Reaper: A Grim Reaper Holiday Adventure

www.riyapresents.com